DANNY BOY

DANNY BOY

JENNY OLDFIELD

Illustrated by
Paul Hunt

Hodder
Children's
Books

a division of Hodder Headline

With thanks to Bob, Karen and Katie Foster, and to the staff and guests at Lost Valley Ranch, Deckers, Colorado

First published in Great Britain in 2000
by Hodder Children's Books

A Catalogue record for this book is available from the British Library

ISBN 0 340 75729 9

Typeset by Avon Dataset Ltd, Bidford-on-Avon, Warks

Printed and bound in Great Britain by
The Guernsey Press Co. Ltd, Channel Isles

Hodder Children's Books
a division of Hodder Headline
338 Euston Road
London NW1 3BH

1

'Involuntary dismount!' Ben Marsh stood up in his stirrups and yelled a warning to the riders behind.

Kirstie reined her palomino, Lucky, to a hasty stop on the steep mountainside. 'What happened? Who came off?'

The new head wrangler swung around, a wry grin visible beneath the broad brim of his dusty stetson. 'Charlie just had a small difference of opinion with the low branch of a ponderosa pine tree!'

'Uh-oh!' Kirstie grinned back. Charlie Miller, the junior wrangler at Half-Moon Ranch, was made of stern stuff. The only thing likely to be hurt by the collision with the tree was his pride.

After all, on this ride Charlie was supposed to be helping Ben to break in one of the new horses, getting the young colt ready to be used eventually by the dudes who visited the remote ranch in the Rockies for their summer vacations. Falling off was not part of the plan!

She urged Lucky on up the slope, waiting for her horse to find firm footholds between the fallen, half-decayed branches and the rocks that pushed up through the loose scree on Bear Hunt Overlook. 'C'mon, boy!' she murmured, watching his ears prick this way and that, then flick round towards her to pay attention to her soft voice. 'Let's go pick Charlie up out of the dirt!'

Slowly Lucky plodded past a grinning Ben, who had just taken out his two-way radio to answer a call from Kirstie's mom, Sandy, back at the ranch.

'You OK, Charlie?' Kirstie and Lucky tackled a sharp bend in the trail around a granite outcrop and almost crashed into the tall, slim, dark figure.

'You bet.' Dusting down his leather chaps and

bending to pick up his stetson, he glanced up into the sun at Kirstie.

'Hey, your face is bleeding!' She pointed to a scratch a couple of inches long across Charlie's cheekbone. There were beads of scarlet and a thin trickle leading towards his chin.

'Ain't nothing.' He wiped the wound with the back of his gloved hand. 'Did you see my darned horse?'

'Nope. He didn't come back down my way. Must've gone on ahead. What did he do; buck you off?' Kirstie scanned the upper slopes of the Overlook, a pinprick of anxiety scratching the surface of her good mood as she realised that the new horse was still loose. This was wild country, more than eight miles from base, with jagged peaks and dangerous ledges to contend with. And it was Danny Boy's first outing along the tough route.

Charlie shook his head. 'I was asking him to squeeze past the tree on the right hand side, but at the last split second he preferred the left. He did a smart piece of footwork that left me hanging from that there branch!'

Pressing her lips together to bring her grin

under control, Kirstie stuck to the serious job of seeking out the young horse between the tall, rough-barked ponderosa pines.

She was looking for a small, wiry colt of three and a half years, loose limbed and skinny. Black from the tip of his ears to the base of his hooves, except for a dazzling white star on his forehead, Danny Boy would be hard to spot in amongst the deep shadows cast by the trees and rocks.

'Loose horse bushwhacking back down the slope!' a rider called from down below.

'Uhh!' Charlie sagged and groaned as he recognised Hadley Crane's voice. 'This ain't my day!'

Not only was Ben there to witness his fall from grace, but old Hadley too. Hadley, the ex-head wrangler, with a lifetime's knowledge of horses and the broken bones and old scars to prove it. Though he was officially retired from his job of managing Sandy Scott's trail horses, he'd come along today for the ride.

'It's OK; I got him!' another voice called as Kirstie backed Lucky around the hairpin bend and let Charlie through.

'That's Matt on Cadillac,' she told the red-faced

young wrangler. 'Looks like he cut across Danny Boy's path and grabbed his rein!'

Charlie nodded, then slid and skidded down the hillside in a cloud of dust to retrieve his horse from Matt. Soon he was remounted and ready to go.

'That black colt's a handful,' Hadley remarked, coming up alongside Ben with Kirstie listening in. She knew the old ranch hand would do his usual trick of testing out and judging the newcomer.

'Sure is,' Ben agreed easily, hitching his radio on to his belt and heading on along the Overlook. By this time, the whole group was pushing on up the mountain towards Eagle's Peak. 'That's why the last place sold him: the Crooked Z, over at San Luis. Too much spirit, they reckoned. Head wrangler there, guy named Jess Robbins, said Danny had an awkward streak that no amount of working with him would put right.'

That's the way to handle Hadley! Kirstie said to herself with a smile. *Be up front. Don't let him get under your skin!*

Hadley's silence, as he edged Crazy Horse through a narrow squeeze between two tall, black rocks, spoke volumes. He rode stooped in the saddle, hat pulled well forward, red kerchief protecting the back of his neck from the fierce sun's rays.

'I didn't agree.' Ben went on putting his point of view. 'In my opinion, Danny Boy is a fine little quarter-horse. Typical mix of old Spanish mustang and Irish stallion. Good conformation: short, strong back, short head, muscular body. Great knees.'

Kirstie turned around to check these points as the head wrangler ran through them. What she saw fitted in with Ben's description; Danny was neat. And, yep; he had good, flat knees.

'A horse can look fine, but it's his temperament that counts.' Hadley pushed Ben a little harder.

'Ain't nothing wrong with Danny's temperament that a little hard work won't iron out,' Ben insisted, falling back from Hadley to wait for Charlie and Matt.

Which left Kirstie and Lucky riding alongside Hadley and Crazy Horse.

'That boy has an ornery streak!' Hadley muttered.

Kirstie laughed. 'Why am I thinking here of pots calling kettles black?'

The stubborn old man pursed his thin lips. 'I ain't saying it's a bad thing,' he countered. 'A little orneriness gets a cowboy a long way—'

'So why not the same with a horse?' Kirstie cut in, the sun full on her face as they rode out of the trees on to a wide open slope looking down to Big Bear River. She breathed deep and joined forces with Ben over the prickly question of cute little Danny Boy. 'Give me a colt with personality any day!'

Glancing round at Danny as he trotted out between the spiky yukka plants and bright pink globe-cacti, she suspected that the gleaming black three year old had personality by the bucketload.

It was in the way he picked up his neat hooves and carried his head. There was a liveliness in his big, dark eyes, breeding in his small, velvety muzzle and tidy throat-latch. *That little horse knows his own mind!* Kirstie thought to herself, coaxing Lucky into a trot and then into a lope across the sun-soaked hill. Like she'd said to Hadley, *Give me a horse with a spark, a bit of get-up-and-go!*

'So they mined silver along Miners' Ridge and down there in Big Bear River.'

They were a mile further along the trail, and Kirstie had got the normally uncommunicative Hadley talking on one of his favourite subjects.

'We're talking a hundred and fifty years back, after the fur trappers and hunters had moved through this territory and headed north west.'

She let the drone of Hadley's story drift by, tuned into the amble of Lucky's steps and the sway of his broad back in the midday heat. The group had reached another narrow, rocky section of the trail, with the river rushing through canyons and over waterfalls way down a steep drop to their left and the mountain rising almost sheer to their right. Dimly she was aware of Ben and Matt riding ahead, but most of her concentration was on how Charlie was guiding a reluctant Danny Boy along the unfamiliar track.

'How did they know there was silver in the mountains?' she murmured, glancing down at the white, foaming river.

'Some cowboy letting his horse drink one day, saw a glint of metal on the bank of the river, I reckon.' Hadley's style was slow and easy once he got into the swing. 'He's tired of making a dollar a day driving longhorns, and he's heard a man can get rich quick if he stakes his claim. So he gets himself a pan, a pick an' a shovel and buys himself ten feet of river bed. Breaks his back from dawn till dusk, just surface grubbing, looking for easy pickings.'

'I'd rather herd beeves,' Kirstie chipped in. Riding the range all day on a cow pony that could run like the wind and turn on a silver dollar sounded like heaven to her.

'Mining wasn't an easy life,' Hadley admitted. 'Pretty soon they exhausted the easy pickings and turned to digging shafts right into these hills, looking for the mother lode deep under the rock. Truth is, this part of Eagle's Peak, from Bear Hunt Overlook on, has more holes running through it than Swiss cheese.'

Kirstie sighed at the idea that men should turn their back on the sunlight and tunnel like moles underground. She knew that many had died when the tunnels collapsed and rocks crushed them. Right up ahead, for instance, was Monument Rock; a tall finger pointing skywards, with its own tragic piece of history attached.

'See that!' Hadley jerked his thumb towards the rapids below. He pointed towards a row of rotting sluices that lined the riverbank for a half mile stretch. The wooden chutes stood on rickety stilts, overgrown with willow bushes and young, bright green aspens. 'That's what's left of men's dreams: a heap of old wood.'

He told her that each chute represented one man's claim. 'Most of them are buried under Monument Rock,' he reminded her. 'Worn out and broken by the work – most were lucky if they weren't killed by Indians or starved in a blizzard.'

'Hey, Hadley!' Matt had hung back and overheard the last sentence or two. 'You sure know how to make a person feel good!' He grinned at Kirstie. 'Did he tell you that some of these old miner guys did actually strike it rich?'

'Nope.' Kirstie's grey eyes wrinkled behind a broad smile. Matt was home from vet school for the summer, and the two of them were getting along great. Today, Sunday, was the day when groups of guests switched around; the old ones left and new ones came in. Meanwhile, the staff could find a few hours to relax and ride their own favourite trails.

'Well, here you go!' Matt began his own story, matching Cadillac's long stride to Lucky and

Crazy Horse's pace. 'This is the story of Miner John.

'Miner John is the guy who struck it rich down there along Big Bear River. Dug a shaft some place under Mountain Lion Ridge, found more silver than you can imagine! Every week he rode his old mule, Jethro, into San Luis, tied him to the hitching post outside the post office and strode right in there with a sack full of silver.'

Kirsie nodded and murmured in the right places, enjoying the smell of wild thyme which wafted by on the warm breeze. Matt's story meandered lazily on.

'And every week, a horde of would-be claim jumpers followed John and that old mule back into these hills, ready to follow him every step of the way and grab a share of what he'd legally laid claim to. Only, John was smart. He had a secret route down from Mountain Lion Ridge that only he knew, and every single time those claim jumpers followed him he'd reach a certain point, just by Monument Rock, where he'd turn the corner and vanish. By the time the posse of guys following reached the rock, John and Jethro had disappeared!

'So he protected his claim, no claim jumper ever stole any of his silver, and he just kept on depositing it in a satchel in San Luis Post Office, until—'

'One day, deep in winter, when he tried to cross Big Bear River in full flood, why, he was swept clean off his feet by the raging, icy current and drowned!' Kirstie cut in.

Matt pretended to be amazed. His jaw dropped and he gave her a doleful stare. 'You heard the story already?'

'A million times,' she giggled. 'And to this day, not a single soul knows the exact location of John's mine shaft! Except Jethro, I guess. And no way was he gonna tell!'

'So how was Danny Boy?' Sandy Scott greeted Charlie with the important question of the day.

The group had circumnavigated Eagle's Peak and returned by a lower route which followed Big Bear River back upstream. Where the river met Five Mile Creek, they'd climbed again, until they reached Hummingbird Rock and caught their first sight of Half-Moon Ranch nestled in the next valley.

With home and a good feed in view, Kirstie had felt Lucky pick up his pace. It was the same for the other tired horses. She noticed Charlie struggle to hold Danny back from a full-blooded lope along the final stretch of meadow and heard Hadley mutter dire warnings to Ben that the new horse was already in danger of growing barn sour.

So the lively colt had pretty well answered Sandy's anxious question for them before Charlie could even dismount in the corral. Danny had been ahead of the bunch, sweating and breathing hard, fighting the young wrangler through the tight rein and the bit.

'He was OK,' Charlie muttered, careful to keep his freshly scarred cheek turned away from the ranch boss. 'Needs a little work.'

'He was nutty.' Matt told his mom the truth as he slid from Cadillac's saddle. 'Didn't hardly do a thing he was told!'

'Hmm. Typical teenager.' Sandy piled her fair hair under her hat, then took hold of Danny's reins. 'Lots of muscle, not much common sense!' She glanced at Charlie's cut face and embarrassed look. 'Not your fault,' she reassured him. 'So don't feel bad. Just get that face cleaned up and we'll see you at supper.'

Unsaddling Lucky and lugging his tack into the tack-room, Kirstie got the sense that underneath the calm tone, her mom was worried. 'Danny will be OK,' she told her, coming back with curry comb and brush. She began to brush Lucky's dusty coat until it shone gold again.

The black colt pawed the dirt with a restless hoof, nostrils flared. He tugged at the rein and pulled impatiently towards the closed gate leading down to the creek and Red Fox Meadow beyond.

Sandy held tight and waited for him to settle. 'He's a challenge!'

Looking over Lucky's back at the spirited youngster, a gleam came into Kirstie's eyes. *A challenge; yeah!*

'Mo-om,' she began in a lilting, coaxing voice. 'Y'know I have lots of spare time – no school and all – so why don't you hand Danny over to me for some special one-to-one work?'

Still Danny tossed his head, his mane flying and the white star on his black forehead flashing in the sun.

Sandy stepped quickly out of the way as his

pawing hoof landed close to her own foot. Then she bumped against the hitching rail, lost her balance and let go.

Freedom! Danny Boy felt the reins flap against his neck. He saw the creek and the meadow beyond the closed gate. No time for his cinch to be loosened and saddle to be removed; he was hungry and thirsty, and one hundred yards beyond that gate were food and water!

So he left Sandy stumbling and set off at a trot, swerving between the hitching rails, ignoring Kirstie's cry and Ben's waving arms as he emerged from the tack-room.

'Danny, come back!' Kirstie yelled.

The horse was crazy. He was heading straight for the gate; four feet high and bolted shut.

He had it in his sights, ears pricked, black mane and tail flying. The lope gathered speed, until a couple of paces before the gate, Danny leaned back on his haunches and launched himself into the air.

'Wow, look at that!' Kirstie cried.

Little Danny soared. He raised his knees high and tucked his front hooves under him. His back legs propelled him high into the air.

'He cleared the gate!' Kirstie gasped. 'Did you see that horse jump?'

Beyond the gate, Danny loped on towards the stream. He splashed in up to his knees, raising spray that shone like diamonds in the sun and racing for the green grass beyond.

2

'Oh, Danny Boy, the pipes, the pipes are calling,
Across the glen and up the mountainside . . .'
Matt half-hummed and half-sang an old melody
as he sat astride Cadillac and steadily herded a
bunch of horses from the meadow into the corral.

Dawn light was breaking over the mountains to
the sound of gates clashing, hooves splashing
through the creek and clip-clopping into the dirt
yard, and to the sight of Kirstie and Charlie
already up and about, raking the yard and
fetching tack from the tack-room.

'Who's that for?' Charlie asked Kirstie as he saw her sling an unfamiliar blanket and saddle across a hitching rail. The horn of the saddle was shiny and new, the tooling on the long, broad stirrup leathers intricate.

'It's for Danny Boy!' she told him airily. 'New horse deserves a new saddle, don't you think?'

Shrugging, Charlie went about his business.

'You got a "yes" from the boss, I take it?' Matt swung down from Cadillac and set about putting saddles on horses, ready for the new guests. 'Mom said you could work with Danny?'

'Well, let's just say I didn't get a "no"!' She grinned at her brother, remembering the moment when the plucky little black horse had sailed clear over the gate. In the excitement of discovering that Danny's Irish blood had given him the ability to jump obstacles that most quarter-horses would baulk at, Sandy had forgotten to deliver an answer to her daughter's request.

Before Matt could object, Kirstie slipped under the rail and jogged out of the corral, using the wooden footbridge to cross the creek. There, in Red Fox Meadow, were Yukon, Pepper and

Jitterbug, all tugging alfalfa hay from the metal feeding-crib nearest to the gate. And further off were Snowflake the brown-and-white Appaloosa, Chigger the black-and-white paint, and Taco the little dark bay mare. None of these horses were due to be ridden today, it seemed.

'Hey, Lucky!' Headcollar in hand, Kirstie climbed the white fence and jumped down into the meadow.

Her palomino trotted up willingly, expecting a normal day's work. His blond mane and tail swished like silk; his golden coat shone in the early sun.

'You get time off today; lucky you!' she joked, patting his soft muzzle. 'I came to fetch Danny Boy. Did you see him lately?'

Lucky nickered and blew on her hand. He danced attendance on her as she strode into the field, picking up his hooves and nodding his head.

'There he is!' Kirstie spotted the black horse kicking up his heels and loping along the far fence, obviously not in the mood to be caught. She thought how full of life he looked, mane flying, hooves pounding. And how supple and lithe, with his curved neck and muscular shoulders; a youngster showing off in all his glory.

'OK, Lucky, I need your help!' she murmured, getting her horse to stand still while she slipped her arms around his neck and mounted bareback. Without even a headcollar, just holding lightly to his mane, she pressed with her calves to urge him into a trot. 'Let's show that young Danny a thing or two!'

Lucky understood that the task was to bring in the young newcomer. He broke smoothly into a lope towards the far fence, aiming to corner Danny and give Kirstie time to slip from his back to attach the headcollar. Bigger and stronger than the colt, he soon caught up with him and bossed him to a standstill as Kirstie had hoped.

'Good boy!' she breathed, sliding down to the ground and quietly approaching Danny Boy. 'Now, look here,' she murmured, taking note of the colt's pricked ears and alert stance, 'you and me have some talking to do. I'm the boss around here, OK? You see this collar? Now, I'm gonna slip it around your head nice and easy. You're gonna be a nice boy and come with me.' She slid the halter over his nose and buckled it in one easy movement. 'Yeah, that's great! It didn't hurt none, did it?'

Waiting until Kirstie had completed the task, Lucky then turned and allowed her and Danny Boy out of the corner. He watched them walk across the meadow together, giving a sad little whinny, as if to say to Kirstie, 'How come I'm not your favourite no more?'

She smiled at him over her shoulder. 'Don't give me that sob-stuff! You and I get to ride later, after I've worked Danny Boy in the arena!'

'You checked that with the boss?' This time it was Ben who asked the question. The head wrangler was fetching Johnny Mohawk from the meadow as his mount for the day. Johnny was another lightly built, black horse, with the same kind of free spirit as young Danny Boy.

Kirstie grinned defiantly at Ben and led the way over the bridge into the corral.

'What did or didn't you check with me?' Sandy Scott put in. She'd overheard Ben's remark from inside the barn and came out now to see what Kirstie was up to. 'Uh-oh!' She spotted Danny and recognised right away what her daughter was planning. 'Hey, Kirstie, maybe it would be a good idea to wait until Ben has put in a little more work with the colt.'

'But, Mom . . .' She frowned and hesitated.

'You saw him yesterday. Charlie had a hard time keeping him under control.'

'Yeah, but I don't want to take him out on the trail. I plan to work with him in the arena, doing basic stuff, just getting him to take commands.' Kirstie felt Danny pull away, then quickly change his mind. He turned and stepped towards her, barging her with his head and almost stepping on her toe. 'Quit it, Danny!' she said sharply, digging her elbow into his shoulder and pulling him into line.

Sandy watched thoughtfully. 'What d'you reckon, Ben?'

The head wrangler had just slid the bit into Johnny's mouth and fastened the bridle. Now he too gave some thought to the problem. 'I reckon Kirstie handles a horse just about as good as anyone I know,' he said slowly, his thin face shadowed by the brim of his hat. 'Fact is, if I had to choose someone to work with colts round here, it'd be Kirstie, no doubt about it.'

Kirstie's head went up and her grey eyes shone.

Wow, Ben Marsh had just paid her one big compliment! She thought of all the horse handlers and trainers he must have seen at his old ranch in Wyoming; and yet he was calling her one of the best! 'Thanks, Ben!' she murmured.

He dipped his head in a small nod of acknowledgement.

And her mom took her new head wrangler's opinion on board. 'You heard what the man said,' she told Kirstie, coming up to Danny Boy and putting a steady, slim brown hand on his glossy neck. 'You've got the go-ahead. It's now down to you to turn this pushy hooligan into the best behaved, most docile horse on the ranch!'

'Remember, soft hands and soft eyes!' Ben told Kirstie before he set out with the advanced group of riders up Eagle's Peak trail.

Kirstie was glad of the advice. For, though Ben had expressed confidence in her, she still knew that schooling Danny Boy was going to be a long and difficult task.

'That was the catchphrase of the guy who taught me everything I know about horses. Old-timer named Buster Mayhew over at Echo Basin. And Buster learned all he knew from a guy named Ray Hunt, who is the best colt trainer this side of the Rocky Mountains.'

'So forget all the other experts?' Kirstie had heard of the soft hands and soft eyes method. It meant training the horse to respond to the slightest pressure from your voice and legs, and never over-correcting with the reins.

'Yeah, tune into the horse. Keep one step ahead of him. With a colt like Danny, that's hard to do because he's a smart little guy, not stupid.' Ben warmed up to his theme, letting his normally serious, shy expression grow animated. 'Danny's thinking, thinking all the time. *How can I outwit this little blonde girl who wants to put a bit in my mouth and throw a saddle over my back?*

'*I could try pushing her around a little, showing what a strong guy I am*. That's what he was doing when he tried to step on your foot, but you dug your elbow in just the right place, so he won't try that trick no more.' Ben paused, then turned to walk away towards the bunkhouse across the yard from the corral. 'Wait here!' he instructed. 'I got something in my room you might like to try out with Danny!'

When Ben returned, he was carrying a length of stout rope knotted and looped into what looked to Kirstie like an unusual bridle.

'See this here contraption? This is what we call a bosal. I made it myself; just plaited the horsehair into a rope, so that this knot hangs under the horse's chin, see? And this strip of rawhide goes over his nose.' Ben worked quietly to put the bridle on to Danny as he talked. 'Using a bosal means we don't need a bit because we get all the pressure we need from the noseband, and there ain't a horse in the world likes having his air supply threatened by pressure on his nose. There again, the bosal is softer and kinder than most metal bits in the mouth.'

'And you reckon it'll work good with Danny?' Kirstie was intrigued.

'Try it,' was Ben's answer.

'Hey, Ben, we ever gonna reach Eagle's Peak this side of next week?' Matt called. He was waiting with a group of four riders, all eager to set off on the trail before the hot sun got up.

So Kirstie was left to lead Danny Boy into the

empty arena, where she mounted cautiously and walked him until they both got used to the bosal. She reined him this way and that, got him to go in a figure of eight by slight shifts of weight, drew him to a halt by tugging gently on the plaited reins.

'Nice work,' a voice said from beyond the rail fence.

It was the first Kirstie knew that she had an audience. Glancing up, she saw Hadley's lean figure dressed in a red checked shirt and tall-crowned white stetson. '*Hot* work!' she grinned. 'Hey, Hadley, did you see this bosal contraption of Ben's?'

'Hmm.' Hadley's standard reply indicated that he wasn't impressed.

'*I* like it!' she insisted. 'And so does Danny!'

Her little horse had soon learned that pressure on the noseband was a signal for him to respond to leg and voice commands. His ears were pricked and flicking in all directions; his step was lively, ready to move from walk into trot. After the severe feel of cold metal across his tongue, he obviously preferred Ben's home-made alternative.

So, with Hadley's beady eye on them, Kirstie

moved Danny Boy through his paces, working for an hour or more until the heat began to beat down on her shoulders, through the thin layer of her cotton shirt. By this time, she'd got Danny to turn and stop with ease, even at a lope, without any sign of the nuttiness that he'd displayed out on the trail the previous day.

'Yeah, nice work.' Hadley spoke for the first time in ages. 'Maybe give the horse a rest now, though.'

'Hmm.' Kirstie pursed her lips and glanced around. If she was perfectly honest, she was a little disappointed that Danny had given her so few problems. It was like she'd said to Hadley yesterday: *Give me a colt with personality any day!* So she ignored his advice now and decided to put Danny through one more test. 'Let's see how you jump those low rails in the yard with me in the saddle!' she urged, turning him out of the arena and pointing him towards the fence which bordered the ranch house lawn.

Danny saw the rails and his ears pricked up. He ignored the fact that Matt's car was parked nearby and that the lawn beyond the rails was currently being sprinkled by turning jets of clear water. *Rails!* was all he thought.

'Steady, boy!' Kirstie began to regret her decision. She felt him bunch up, ready to fly at the jump.

What d'you mean, steady? You want me to jump? Boy, will I jump! Danny broke from a trot across the yard into a full-throttle gallop.

'Whoa!' She pulled at the reins but the colt raced through the pressure on the noseband. 'Not that way, Danny; we're gonna get . . .'

He came to the rail, soared and cleared it by a mile. He landed under the sprinkler as it swung round towards them.

'. . . Wet!' Kirstie yelled. Soaked to the skin by cool, clear drops!

'. . . And he stopped dead under that sprinkler, and refused to move an inch!' Kirstie recounted the story to her best friend, Lisa Goodman. 'His attitude was: "I like it under here. It's good and cool!" And no amount of me persuading him was gonna make him change his mind!'

'Hey, you in front; keep the noise down!' an irritated voice called.

Kirstie and Lisa were in Mineville for the evening to see a movie. Lisa's grandfather, Lennie Goodman, had driven them into town, dropped them off at the picture house, then gone on to call in at the mining museum to chat with an old friend, the curator, Gus McDonald.

The only problem was, Kirstie's head was too full of Danny Boy to be able to concentrate on the sci-fi blockbuster that was playing on screen.

'His new saddle was dripping wet!' she whispered. 'Not to mention my hat and shirt. And I got no sympathy from Hadley, I can tell you!'

'Sshh!' A hand tapped Kirstie on the shoulder and warned her to be quiet.

For a few minutes, she and Lisa squished down in their seats and watched aliens zap each other out of the skies.

'Danny Boy's gonna be great, though!' Kirstie leaned sideways to hiss in Lisa's ear. 'He's one smart horse, and real pretty. You'll see when you next come visit. You'll pick him out easy; he's the all-black colt with a white star. And, man, can he jump!'

'OK, enough!' This time the picture house manager came sternly down the aisle. 'Either you two girls quit talking, or you vacate the premises.'

Lisa gulped a mouthful of popcorn. 'What d'you wanna do?' she muttered at Kirstie.

Kirstie took one more look at the space wars saga – *Zap! Vroom! Zappp!* – 'Vacate the premises!' she mouthed back at her friend.

Sitting eating a Big Mac, describing to Lisa all Danny's little quirks – how he preferred the bosal to the bit, how he would jump anything you pointed him toward – was better by far than watching million dollar special effects on the screen.

'You know something? You're obsessed!' Lisa teased her between bites of burger. 'Danny this,

Danny that! I never knew a person so crazy about horses!'

'Yeah, but I got plans for him!' Kirstie insisted. Outside, the street lights were beginning to glow and all the neon signs just starting to flicker into life. 'I'm gonna work him some more in the arena; maybe a week or ten days. Then I'm gonna start riding him out on the trails, easy ones first to get him used to being with a group and to teach him some manners. Then we get to go on the high trails, up Miners' Ridge, along Bear Hunt Overlook!'

'Crazy!' Lisa said again, with a laugh.

Pausing for breath, Kirstie laughed back. 'Yeah, crazy,' she admitted. Her enthusiasm for the little black colt had just got them thrown out of a movie, for goodness sake. She felt a warm, proud glow as she remembered the progress he'd already made. 'But good-crazy, not bad-crazy!'

Lisa's grin spread from ear to ear. 'Crazy-crazy!' she insisted. 'Kirstie Scott is totally, one hundred per cent mad about her horse!'

3

Kirstie's patient plan to bring Danny Boy to the point where he would be ready for dude visitors to ride went smoothly throughout July and August.

They progressed from the arena to the trails, starting off with the easy Five Mile Creek ride, where Danny had to learn the rules of trail riding under Ben's direction.

'Don't let him overtake another horse at a competitive gait,' the wrangler reminded Kirstie when he saw Danny try to barge his way past a guest riding Snowflake. 'He has to learn to keep in line.'

This was a difficult lesson for the lively little horse, who always wanted to be up front. Kirstie used the bosal to steady him and keep him back, praising him when he accepted the command.

'And no eating!' Ben reined Hollywood Princess to come up alongside greedy Danny. The colt had a four foot length of tobacco-plant stalk clenched between his strong teeth.

Kirstie promised to keep him away from temptation in future.

'Real important; don't let Danny break into a trot as we head for home,' Ben instructed at the end of the first outing. He'd seen the youngster straining at the reins, plunging into the creek, then up the far bank, his mind set on being first back to the ranch. 'A barn-sour trail horse ain't no good to us,' he warned. 'So keep him in check, OK!'

Kirstie sighed as the head wrangler rode off on his glamorous grey mare. Hollywood Princess was a star; an American Albino with Arab features who loved to be the centre of attention. She glided along with the smoothest possible gait; a dazzling white picture of pure elegance.

'Hey, cowboy up!' Charlie grinned at her from further along the trail. 'Why the long face? You and Danny are doing great!'

'Thanks.' She appreciated the young wrangler's encouragement, but somehow she felt down. Maybe it was from looking at the lovely Hollywood Princess. Smart as he was, Danny would never reach that level of attention-grabbing perfection.

Want to bet? As if by telepathy, Danny Boy picked up his rider's dejected mood. He felt he had something to prove to her. OK, so he knew now not to push his way to the front of the line, or to lope for home. But had they told him not to jump the log coming up ahead? He saw the thick, felled tree at the bottom of a forestry team track and set his sights on clearing it.

Kirstie felt him liven up. His muscles bunched as he set himself towards the tree trunk.

So, I might not rate high in the glamour department, he seemed to be telling the others as Hollywood Princess sashayed by. *But looks ain't everything, believe me!*

'OK, Danny, let's try!' Kirstie whispered. She

pressed her heels into his sleek sides.

Small horse, big obstacle. Short legs and a height of three feet, a span of six or eight to clear. Answering Kirstie's command, Danny let rip at the log. His hooves thundered across the dry, yellow grass, the log looming large before them.

With split-second timing Kirstie rose out of the saddle. Danny soared. He landed fair and square on the far side of the log. Then he loped in a wide arc, back to the bunch of spectators.

'Yee-hah!' Charlie set up a cry of approval. 'Nice jump, Kirstie!'

'Oo-aah!' Several guests joined in. 'See that little horse go!'

Soon everyone was cheering. Danny's head was held high in a cocky attitude that said, 'Thanks, but there was nothing to it!'

'Hmm.' Ben was the only one not joining in the applause. Instead, he gave Kirstie a touch of the old Hadley treatment.

Did 'Hmm' mean, 'Fine, but don't let Danny Boy show off in future'? Or did it mean, 'Nice work!'?

Probably a bit of both, Kirstie decided.

But she was glad for Danny. His first time out

since their one-to-one sessions, and he'd shown he could shine bright as any Hollywood star!

Then there was work on the steeper trails. Throughout September, Danny proved to be a hard worker on the rocky upper slopes of the Meltwater Range, slogging his way along ridges and up narrow canyons.

And he had stamina. One day, just before the first snow of the year was due, he made it all the way to Monument Rock without taking a rest. Hadley was in the small group of expert riders who had come this far, pointing out to Charlie the very tree where he and Danny Boy had had their difference of opinion, ending in Charlie's involuntary dismount.

'Yeah, thanks for reminding me of that, Hadley!' The young wrangler blushed and pushed Crazy Horse on ahead towards Mountain Lion Ridge. 'I'm going to find me Miner John's silver mine!' he called back to Kirstie with a wry grin. 'When I strike it rich, I won't have to take no more hassle from Hadley!'

'Good luck!' she hollered.

Crazy Horse was a shambling, poorly-put-together joke of a mount; sway backed, with a big, ugly face on him. But he was a loyal, sure-footed old guy and Charlie, for one, loved him. On a whim, Kirstie decided to follow the two of them and join them in their get-rich-quick quest for precious metal.

'We came past the old sluice boxes a while back,' she reminded Charlie, pointing down into the valley towards the fast-running river and the series of small waterfalls. 'What we need to find is the spot where old John used to vanish behind a rock; it most likely leads to a tunnel where he hid until the claim-jumpers gave up trying to follow him and went back home.'

Charlie nodded. He let Crazy Horse poke around in the undergrowth, amongst paintbrush cacti with their plumes of scarlet flowers. 'Yeah, but I got a problem with that,' he remarked.

'Which is?' Kirstie and Danny Boy searched between tall rocks and in and out of small copses of aspen trees.

'Which is that John's tunnel must be the best hidden, most secret passage in this whole range of mountains, considering the fact that, week after week, for years on end he managed to throw off bunches of silver-hungry guys!'

'We need a map!' Kirstie decided. 'A map that marks the spot with a big black cross and the words "John's Mine". Like that exists!'

Failing that, they both decided to abandon their search for instant wealth. They rejoined the group on the ridge and plodded onwards, circumnavigating Eagle's Peak and coming down the mountain as before.

'You've done a good job with Danny.' With Half-Moon Ranch in view in the valley, Ben rode level with Kirstie.

Something in his manner told her that he'd reached a decision. She listened quietly, trying to squash down a mixed-bag of emotions; pride and sadness, satisfaction and yet a strong longing to hang on to Danny for as long as she could.

'I knew when I bought him he'd be a great ranch horse, and now you've put the work in with him, I can see I was right. Mind, it ain't every dude we get here who could safely ride him.'

'Yeah, I know. What Danny needs is an advanced lady rider; someone who can handle him.'

'Not too rough,' Ben agreed.

'A woman who can sit the saddle pretty good. She'll need to jump him too. Danny likes to jump, remember.'

'I remember.' Ben smiled. 'So anyways, Kirstie, I'm thinking about the next bunch of guests we get in later today—'

'Do you think he's really ready?' she cut in, suddenly afraid. 'Maybe he needs a little more work!'

'He's ready,' Ben insisted. He glanced at her, then smiled kindly. 'Hard to let go, ain't it?'

She nodded.

'But listen up; the horse has to start to earn his keep. I have to put his name on the list for guests to ride.'

'OK.' Her heart felt like lead, yet she should have been pleased. After all, this was what they'd been working for.

'He'll still be around,' Ben reminded her. 'And you gotta be proud of the way he turned out.'

'I am,' she sighed. 'It's OK, Ben, I know you're right. Danny's ready for work, aren't you, boy?'

The black horse tossed his head and snorted, picking his way confidently along the narrow ridge, with the white water rushing over rocks sixty feet below.

Ben narrowed his eyes and gave her a satisfied nod. 'Good work, Kirstie. And you know, most of all you owe it to Danny Boy to say your goodbyes and let him go!'

It was misty when Kirstie went out to the corral first thing next morning, and there was a frost on the ground. Zipping up her jacket and slipping her hands inside a sturdy pair of buckskin gloves, she found Ben at work straightening up the blackboard where he listed riders' names alongside the names of all the horses in the Half-Moon ramuda.

First off, he dusted away last week's guests, ready to fill the gaps with new visitors after he'd given them their introductory talk. Then Kirstie saw him take a piece of chalk and add a new name to the list on the left-hand side.

'Danny Boy'. There he was; an official Half-Moon Ranch horse!

'Proud moment!' Sandy Scott said, coming up behind Kirstie and giving her shoulder a quick squeeze.

'Yeah!' She stayed a long time staring at the name, wondering exactly who would get to ride Danny, hoping that he or she would be skilled enough to follow the 'soft hands and soft eyes' style of horsemanship.

'You know we got a convention of vacation company delegates visiting us this week?' Kirstie's mom called briskly from the tack-room. 'It's kinda important. If these guys like the place, they'll include us in their brochures for next summer.'

'And that means we get a whole heap of new business!' Matt appeared in the doorway, armed with brushes and curry combs which he dumped in Kirstie's arms. 'So get working!' he ordered. 'We want those horses all spruced up and ready to go by the time these dudes have eaten breakfast!'

By eight o'clock, Kirstie's arms were aching from the brushing of dusty coats, tangled manes and tails. By eight-thirty, all the saddles had to be on.

She slung blanket pads over the horses' backs, eased on the heavy saddles, then tightened cinches.

'Who checked bridles this morning?' Ben called, striding across the corral with paperwork from the office.

'I did,' Charlie shouted back, running from the barn with headcollars slung over his shoulder.

'Three still dirty!' The head wrangler found fault over details.

'I'll clean them.' Kirstie stepped in, glad to be kept busy. Pretty soon those guests would show up at the rail and the allocating of horses would begin. She'd purposefully kept Danny Boy out of her line of vision, preferring that Matt should bring out his smart saddle and prepare him for his first day of real work.

She went into the tack-room to polish the metal bits and wipe the leather bridles, and when she came out again on to the porch, she found a dozen guests already gathered around Ben, eager to discover who was to be their horse.

'You ridden before?' the wrangler asked each in turn.

'Nope. This is my first time!' a guy with a small dark moustache and close cropped hair cheerfully admitted.

'Well, Tony, I'd say Crazy Horse was a good

choice for you. Nice and steady. He's what we call kid-broke.'

'Sounds good to me!' The easy-going guest went off with Charlie to be introduced to his horse.

'Hey, Cheryl!' Relaxing into the routine, Ben addressed a nervy looking woman dressed in a heavy cream fleece jacket, a brand new black stetson and expensive sunglasses. 'How 'bout you? You ridden before?'

'Twice when I was a kid,' Cheryl admitted with a scared laugh. 'You give me a nice gentle horse, you hear!'

Ben reassured her and told her that Yukon, a brown-and-white paint, would be the ideal ride for her.

'Hey, and you must be Lorena!' he said to an attractive, flame-haired woman who stood next in line.

'Lorena May Brown,' she confirmed. 'And before you ask; yeah, sure I know how to ride. I've been learning English at a place in New York state.'

Ben smiled and nodded. 'Well, Lorena May, we ride western here. Is that gonna be a problem for you?'

'Hell, no!' The woman shrugged off Ben's concerns. She had a flirty manner and a low, sexy voice. 'English, western; it don't make no difference to me, honey. I've been riding since I was five years old!'

Shy Ben backed off from Lorena's fluttering lashes and husky drawl. 'Say, maybe you'd like to ride Danny Boy,' he suggested, as if the idea had flown at him and he'd grabbed it fast.

Oh no; not Lorena May! To Kirstie, still standing in the porch nearby, this sounded all wrong. Sure, she was the right height and weight, and she said she could ride. But what if she was overplaying her experience? With her mascara and her curtain of long red hair sweeping across her face, she didn't exactly look the outdoor type.

'Danny Boy!' The name seemed to appeal to the glamorous guest.

And to Kirstie's annoyance, Matt stepped in to show Lorena the horse. He led her to where the black colt was tethered, telling her that Danny had personality-plus.

'He's cute,' the woman agreed. She patted the horse's neck and looked him up and down.

Cute! Kirstie frowned. *Danny's better than cute!*

45

'He can be a little hard to handle because he's young and fresh,' Matt explained, setting it out as a challenge to Lorena May.

'Young and fresh I like!' she teased, flirting now with Matt and forgetting all about Danny.

'Problem?' Charlie passed Kirstie and noticed the dark looks flitting across her face.

'Look who they put on Danny!' she said fiercely.

Charlie assessed the slim figure dressed in lightweight denims and fancy turquoise boots. 'I give her five minutes down the trail,' he predicted. 'Soon as the first snowflakes fall, she'll be turning Danny around and heading back home!'

'Snow?' Kirstie echoed.

Charlie nodded. 'Forecast for the area south west of Denver above ten thousand feet.'

'That's us sure enough.' Maybe Charlie was right; the bad weather would soon put off the likes of Lorena May Brown, who looked like she would be more at home on a beach in Bermuda than riding Five Mile Creek trail.

'Good!' Kirstie grunted with satisfaction and turned back into the tack-room.

Jealous? Her? *No way!* she would have said.

It was simply that she didn't believe Lorena would be able to handle Danny Boy. Straight, down-to-earth technical judgement; nothing to do with the fact that faithless Danny had nuzzled right up to his new rider and leaned his head against her shoulder. As far as Kirstie was concerned, it was irrelevant that Lorena had immediately thrown both arms around him and given that throaty chuckle.

'Hey, Kirstie, shouldn't you be out here with the advanced group?' Ben stuck his head around the door to look for her.

'Huh. Hmm.' She pretended to look for something she'd lost.

'Was that yes or no?'

'What? Yeah, I guess so!' Grabbing her hat, she stamped outside and strode across the corral to untie Lucky.

The palomino stood, head down and dejected.

'Yeah, I know; it's gonna snow!' Kirstie muttered as she mounted into the saddle. She glanced up at the dark clouds gathering over the jagged horizon, then across at Matt giving Lorena May a leg-up into Danny Boy's saddle. 'It's cold and it's windy. You're right, Lucky; this morning's ride ain't gonna be no fun at all!'

4

'Well, it snowed!' Charlie greeted Kirstie cheerfully as she arrived back at the ranch.

She shook the thin white covering off her yellow slicker and from the brim of her hat. Then she swung her freezing leg over Lucky's saddle to dismount. Teeth chattering, she led the palomino into the shelter of the stalls beside the barn.

'So?' Charlie demanded, following her out of the light, whirling flakes.

Kirstie sniffed and wiped the melting snow from her face. 'So?' she stalled.

'So how did Lorena May go on Danny Boy?'

Deep breath, count to ten. 'Well, you were wrong about her turning back on account of the weather.'

'Yeah?' Genuinely surprised, Charlie looked out up the track that led to Meltwater Trail. 'Say, is that her and Danny just riding in now?'

'Could be.' Kirstie turned her back in an offhand way. She went for a special scoop of food for Lucky; his reward for putting up with the bad conditions. The palomino munched the grain from the palm of her hand.

'Hey, yeah, and she looks like she's having a great time!' Making out that Lorena May was deep in conversation with Matt Scott, Charlie's eyebrows practically shot off the top of his head. 'C'mon, Kirstie, what's the deal with this lady? Can she ride as good as she says?'

'Guess so.' She sniffed again, bending to loosen Lucky's cinch and remove his saddle.

In fact, Lorena May Brown had turned out to be an excellent horsewoman. She rode in the western saddle English style, posting the trot better than any of the wranglers round here could; probably better than Kirstie herself if she was honest. And she wasn't nearly as giddy and girly as she looked. Full of surprises, when the first flakes of snow had fallen, Lorena May had simply turned up the collar of her thin coat and cowboyed up!

'And?' Charlie insisted.

'And what?'

'How did she handle Danny Boy?'

'Good,' Kirstie said through gritted teeth.

To be more specific, the guest had tuned into the young horse's wavelength from the start. She knew just how much pressure to give him with her legs, how much slack in the reins, and when to be stern. In return, Danny had behaved like a gentleman; with perfect manners, willing, yet still plucky and spirited. No, Kirstie couldn't pick the smallest fault in the way her beloved little horse had been handled.

And now Lorena May and Matt rode into the corral, chatting loudly about the advantages of riding English style, ignoring the three or four inches of snow that covered the long barn roof and which was already drifting against the tack-room porch. The wind caught the light flakes in

51

rapid flurries which flew in the faces of both horses and riders.

When Lorena saw Charlie and Kirstie watching her, she immediately cried out. 'Hey, Kirstie! Matt tells me you're the one who just finished working with this colt.'

Feeling her colour rise, Kirstie nodded. She went and held Danny's head as the excited rider dismounted, showering snow from her jacket on to Kirstie.

'Well, honey, let me tell you you did an absolutely great job! He's the sweetest little guy! I tell you, I've had me the most perfect time on the trail with him. Ask your brother here; Danny and I got on fabulously!'

'Thanks.' Kirstie's stammered reply seemed too little. But Lorena's unexpected enthusiasm left her tongue-tied. Clearing her throat in embarrassment, she took Danny under shelter in the stall next to Lucky's.

'Gee, this is such a neat place!' Lorena gushed. 'I just love the space and the fresh air! Just you wait until I write my report. I'm gonna give y'all four diamonds; that's our top rating at Flyaway Vacations!'

'Wow, thanks!' Matt grinned and gave Sandy a thumbs-up sign across the yard. 'Hey, listen, Lorena, why not run up to your cabin and take a dip in the hot tub before you come back down to eat? Kirstie here will take care of Danny for you.'

Still chatting, Matt and Lorena walked away.

Kirstie stared daggers after them. 'Don't – say – a – word!' she warned Charlie, mocking the visitor's gushing drawl. ' "Well, honey . . . he's the sweetest little guy!" '

'Hey!' he grinned. He watched the sway of Lorena May's hips and the tumble of her long red hair as she took off her hat and shook it free. 'I like her!' he insisted. 'Ain't no law against a horsewoman wearing a nice perfume and looking good, is there?'

'Lorena May is great fun!' Sandy said to Kirstie more than once during the early days of the week.

'That Lorena May; she sure can sit a saddle!' Ben told her. Lorena May-this, Lorena May-that.

'Did you see Lorena May jump the creek up by Aspen Falls yesterday afternoon?' Charlie asked admiringly.

It was Wednesday, and Kirstie was sick and tired

of hearing the woman's name. 'Lorena May didn't jump the creek,' she bickered. 'Danny Boy did.'

'Yeah, whatever.' Charlie rolled his eyes at Matt, who was saddling up the horses for a special ride over to Jim Mullins' place. The rancher had called Sandy the night before to ask if any of her advanced guests fancied joining in the fall round-up of his cattle on the Lazy B.

'You should be glad that Danny has a good rider.' Matt reminded Kirstie of some of the nightmare guests who could've ridden the little horse. 'You remember the woman from Dallas? Looked a million dollars with her black leather chaps and fancy jacket. But her idea of riding was to get on the horse and kick him to pieces. Then there was the lady dentist from Pennsylvania; she more or less crucified a horse's mouth by pulling so hard on the reins.'

'Yeah, I know.' Kirsie acknowledged that she ought to be grateful for Lorena May Brown. 'I just wish . . .'

'What?' Matt dumped a pile of blankets in her arms and told her to get busy. He winked at Charlie; a signal that they both knew what was the matter with her.

'I wish . . .' *Let's face it; I wish I could've kept Danny as my very own horse!* The thought stopped her in her tracks.

No, that wouldn't have been right. No way could her mom afford to buy horses that wouldn't earn their keep. And what about Lucky? How would he have felt if Kirstie had shifted her affections on to Danny full-time? How selfish could you get? She sighed and muttered, 'No, forget it.'

And by the time they were ready to set off for the neighbouring ranch, Kirstie had talked herself round into being especially nice to Lorena May. She personally saddled Danny Boy and led him to the flame-haired guest. She held his head as Lorena mounted, then checked his cinch.

'So today we city slickers get to be real cowboys!' Enthusiastic as ever, Lorena May glanced up at the clear blue sky.

'Jim Mullins has cattle up on Miners' Ridge,' Kirstie told her. 'His ranch hands are pretty stretched to try and bring them all in before the snow gets bad.'

'Oh, but it won't snow today!' Lorena gestured towards the cloudless horizon.

'Don't bet on it,' Ben told her in passing. 'Say, would you like to borrow a slicker, Lorena? That denim jacket won't be no good if the snow does blow in like they predicted on the weather forecast.'

'Hold it right there!' Charlie overheard and dropped what he was doing to run to the bunkhouse for his own yellow waterproof coat. He rolled it tight, then strapped it on to the back of Danny's saddle,

'How about you?' Lorena protested. 'Won't you need it?'

'I'm leading a beginners' ride. if it snows, we'll head for home,' he explained, rechecking what Kirstie had just done.

'Ok, time to ride!' Ben announced. 'Charlie with beginners. Matt with intermediates. Hadley's joining me and Kirstie on the advanced ride. Advanced – this is gonna be a tough all-day trek, starting out from here, up Eagle's Peak Trail on to Miners' Ridge, where we hope to pick up Jim's cows. Then we drive them down into the next valley to the Lazy B.'

Kirstie was about to untether Lucky and mount, when Lorena May gave a little gasp and called her back. 'Oh, honey, guess what I did? I forgot my camera! I left it in the dining room.'

'No problem, I'll go get it.' Kirstie ran to retrieve the camera, handing it to Lorena May just as Ben and Hadley led their group out of the corral.

The guest pocketed it with a smile. 'You're a sweetie! How could I bear to miss all those Kodak moments?'

Kirstie smiled back at her, then gave Danny a pat. He returned the gesture with a small, gentle nudge with his nose. 'I guess this is his first time working with cows,' she told Lorena. 'So he may be a little jumpy.'

But the excited guest was in no mood to take advice. 'Don't you believe it! Danny and I are a great team.'

'But he can be a problem if there's something new going on.' Kirstie wanted to get her message through, even though Lorena was already turning Danny and trotting him out of the corral. She jumped into the saddle and followed quickly.

'Don't you worry about a thing!' Lorena insisted, lengthening Danny's stride to a lope as they took the steep northern route towards

Hummingbird Rock. 'Danny and I are gonna handle those longhorns just fine!'

'Yip-yip-yip! Come along, girls! Yip!' Hadley and two guests drove four cows out of a culvert on to Miners' Ridge.

The reddish-brown animals butted clumsily against the slim silver trunks of aspen trees, shaking the last golden leaves to the ground.

Lorena May reined Danny Boy to a halt, whipped out her camera and clicked away happily.

'Good job!' Ben called as the cattle stumbled into view. After two hours bushwhacking across country, the advanced group had gathered eight cows and three spring calves, making a total of eleven units. He radioed the news to the Lazy B, and took instructions that the volunteer wranglers should split into two groups.

'Jim says there are more units up by Monument Rock for sure,' he told Hadley. 'He'd like some of us to drive this bunch back to the ranch and the rest to ride on after the others.'

'I guess you could drive these ones back while I lead the bunch that heads on.' Hadley volunteered his expert knowledge of both the mountain landscape and of cattle, gained from more than forty years working as a ranch hand in the area.

'Hey, me too! Count me in on Hadley's group!' Lorena May cried, eager to snap more of those Kodak moments.

'OK,' Ben agreed, asking for less adventurous riders who were willing to drive the eleven cows home.

Hands were raised, decisions were made. It turned out that Hadley was to take Kirstie, Lorena May and two guests called Darren and Luke along Bear Hunt Overlook towards the tall finger of rock which dominated the horizon.

'You checked your radio?' Ben asked, glancing up at the sky and noting a cluster of wispy white clouds over Monument Rock.

Hadley confirmed that he had with a brief nod, then gave orders for his small group to begin sweeping the culverts to the right of the Overlook. 'It ain't likely that we'll find cows in there,' he admitted. 'There's better grazing further on, so I reckon that's where they'll be.'

So they set off earnestly, Hadley at the head of

the group on Navaho Joe, Lorena May tucked in close behind.

To their rear, the call of 'Yip-yip!' told Kirstie that Ben's home-bound group were already working their way down the slope.

'. . . You had ramrods earning a hundred dollars a month, then under him came the point drivers, line riders and greenhorns.' Hadley's gruff voice kept Lorena May enthralled as they rode the narrow ledge along Bear Hunt Overlook. 'This was way back in the eighteen hundreds, when a hundred dollars was worth something. Mind, those trail bosses earned their dough the hard way. They had a thousand head of beeves to take care of, and even a small stampede could cost you a couple of days.'

'Fascinating!' Lorena May drank in every word, leaving Danny to pick his way over the difficult terrain. 'And tell me, Hadley, how come the old cowboys took along a guitar on the cattle drives? Was that simply for their own amusement?'

'No, ma'am.' He told her how the songs had been used to lull the cattle at night to keep them from stampeding.

Below, to their left, Kirstie could hear the roar

of Big Bear River tumbling over ledges and thundering through ravines. The water level was up, she noted, probably due to the recent snow melt. Looming ahead was the rock which served as a mournful reminder of lives lost in the scramble for silver.

'Hey!' A sudden cry from Darren, a heavy guy in a brown stetson and green checked jacket, broke through the natural sounds of water and wind. 'Bovines to the right!'

Hadley wheeled Joe around on the narrow ledge and trotted back.

'Oh, gee, no, I'm sorry!' A red-faced Darren emerged from a culvert. 'What I saw down there was deer, not cows!'

The old wrangler nodded tersely. 'Keep looking,' was all he said.

So they rode another mile or two, under the shadow of Monument Rock, where Lorena May took dramatic, moody pictures of Hadley and Navaho Joe, then out along Mountain Lion Ridge.

'So, you actually get lions out here?' Lorena's constant stream of chatter directed itself at Kirstie.

'Some.'

Lorena's eyes widened. 'Oooh, really! And grizzlies?'

'No, ma'am. We do get black bears coming down as far as the ranch, though.'

'Cows!' This time it was a yell from Luke that broke into the conversation.

'Sure?' Hadley turned in the saddle to watch the excited guest disappear down a fresh culvert.

'Yeah, four of 'em!' Luke could be heard crashing amongst bushes, his voice muffled by tall walls of rock. 'Yip-yip! C'mon, girls, let's go!'

'Easy now!' Hadley told Navaho Joe as the horse skittered sideways into Danny's flank. 'We ain't got much space around here. Say, Luke, do you want Kirstie to come in and help you drive 'em out?'

'No need. Here they come!'

There was more crashing and snapping of branches, then the first of four frightened cattle burst out of the narrow culvert on to the ledge. Head lowered, stumbling, she went down on to her knees, then picked herself up and veered off in the opposite direction to Kirstie and the rest.

Then came cows number two and three, driven on by Luke's constant calling. It was a mother and calf, both startled out of their wits, eyes rolling, trampling through sage bushes dangerously close to the long, steep drop to the river below.

'Hold it!' Kirstie cried to Luke. The cattle needed time to get their bearings then join the first one, which was by now heading back towards Monument Rock

'Hey, what a great picture!' Lorena May edged Danny closer towards the panicky creatures before Hadley or Kirstie could warn her against it. Close to the exit from the culvert, she let go of the reins and sat, camera poised, waiting for the perfect moment.

The fourth and last cow crashed out of the narrow ravine. Face to face with Danny and his rider, her head went down, threatening him with her long, curved horns.

'Watch out!' Kirstie yelled.

'Yip-yip!' Unable to see the crisis on the ledge, Luke drove the cow from behind.

'No, wait!' Kirstie's pleas were drowned in the cow's bellow. Pressed from both directions, she charged.

Lorena May dropped her camera and plunged

forward to grab the reins. Her shift of weight made Danny stumble, right in the path of the heavy, charging cow.

Lorena's scream pierced the air. As Danny went down, so she was flung sideways, clear of the saddle. She landed against a rock and slid to the ground, lying dead still.

But Danny was on his feet again, rearing up on the narrow track, hooves flailing, teeth bared.

The cow ran directly beneath the horse, bruising her way through by sheer size and weight, regardless of the lethal hooves. Danny came down on top of her, screaming out a high, wild whinny. For a moment, they locked together, horns goring at Danny's belly and chest, hooves thundering down.

Then they twisted apart. The cow used her weight to heave Danny off. She swerved and escaped after the others. But in the struggle Danny lost his footing. As the cow slid away, so his back feet slipped over the edge of the narrow platform, down the slope of loose stones and grit.

'Danny!' Kirstie cried. She darted to seize his rein, to drag him back before he slid out of reach.

Too late. Her fingers clutched dirt; he was

sliding, sliding from view through bushes, over rocks, churning up loose stones and peppering them down the mountain into the roaring river.

Down he went, legs flailing, neck twisted as he tried to protect his head from crashing against the rocks. His helpless, sliding body raised a cloud of grey dust as it gathered speed. Then, for a second, as a stirrup strap caught in the branch of a pine tree, he slowed, skewed around and stopped.

'Oh yes, please, please!' Kirstie whispered.

Then the strap snapped and Danny's downward slide continued.

Kirstie's heart thumped and missed a beat. She watched him through a dust cloud that choked her and stung her eyes. He struggled one last time as he reached a second flat ledge of grey rock. But there was nothing to prevent his fall; the force of gravity went on dragging him down, over the ledge and out of sight into oblivion.

5

'What do we do?' Darren appealed to Hadley in the silence that followed Danny Boy's disappearance over the edge of the cliff. He'd dismounted and run across to the spot where Lorena May lay unconscious.

Luke too jumped down from his horse and crouched at the injured woman's side.

'Danny!' Kirstie murmured, standing at the edge of the ridge, choked by rising dust, her face streaked with tears.

'Kirstie, take the radio. Contact your mom, tell

her we need an ambulance!' Hadley's calm voice broke through her distress. 'Get her to bring the paramedics up the forest ranger's track to Red Eagle Lodge. We'll try and make a stretcher for Miss Brown and meet them there!'

'Do you think we should move her?' Darren asked anxiously as the old ranch hand ran to join them. 'Wouldn't it be better not to touch her and get a chopper out here with a doctor on board?'

'Maybe.' Refusing to commit himself until he discovered the extent of the damage, Hadley tested for a pulse on Lorena May's neck and satisfied himself that she was breathing normally. 'Let me have your jacket,' he instructed Darren. 'First off, we gotta keep her warm ... Kirstie, how're you doing?'

'Mom's not answering!' Though Sandy always wore her radio clipped on to her belt, it was possible that the terrain and weather conditions had weakened the signal so that it wasn't getting through.

'Keep trying! And come away from that edge!'

'Hey, look, she moved!' Luke broke in, pointing to the concussed rider.

Hadley pleaded for space, pushing Darren and

Luke away as Lorena May turned her head and opened her eyes. She peered out from under the thick jacket, her face pale, with a poppy-coloured bruise forming down the left-hand side.

'Mom, please answer!' Kirstie shut her eyes and prayed. At last, the crackle and hiss of the radio cleared and Sandy's voice came through.

'Sandy Scott to Hadley. You got a problem up there? Over!'

'Mom, it's not Hadley, it's me! Yeah, there's been an accident. We need an ambulance up at Red Eagle Lodge. That's right, isn't it, Hadley? We're gonna make it over to meet the ambulance?'

The old man sat back on his haunches and nodded.

'OK, I got that, Kirstie. Leave it to me. But tell me quick; who got hurt? Over.'

'Lorena!' she replied, her voice breaking down. 'Over.'

'Anyone else? Over.'

'And Danny!' she sobbed. 'Oh, Mom, he fell from Mountain Lion Ridge, right over the edge of an overhang!'

'Did he hit the water?' Sandy wanted to know.

'We couldn't see! I don't think he did. We'd have made him out if he'd ended up in the river, wouldn't we?' She would have seen him plunge into the rapids, his dark head bobbing to the surface, and would have had to stand by helpless as the cruel current had swept him away.

'Yes, most likely. Listen, honey, I can hear you're taking it hard, but hold on. Try not to think the worst. If you didn't see exactly what happened to Danny, then what we have to do is send a couple of people down there to find out. That's after we get Lorena May out of there, OK? I said OK? Over!'

'OK,' she echoed faintly. Her mom's words had rekindled a small hope. Maybe, just maybe there was a chance that Danny had survived the fall. 'Mom, radio for Matt and Charlie to come quick as they can. Tell them to bring ropes and a veterinary kit. Over!'

'I'll do that. Kirstie, you help Hadley all you can. Take good care of Lorena.'

During this last message, the signal had begun to crackle and break up again, so Kirstie clicked off the radio and ran to see what she could do for Hadley.

'Darren and Luke are searching out two strong, straight branches to make a stretcher,' he explained. 'We'll tie a couple of jackets between them to form a cradle. Lorena here ain't heavy. We should be able to carry her easy.'

'How are you doing?' Kneeling by the injured woman, Kirstie spoke softly.

'I've been better,' came the shaky reply. Lorena lay half propped against the rock where she'd fallen, still pale but managing a rueful smile.

'What hurts?'

'My leg mostly. Hadley reckons I broke it. He says he'll try to splint it and strap it up before they carry me.'

Kirstie nodded. 'But you can move everything else – your arms, your back?'

'Yeah. Lucky, huh? Could've been my spine; my neck even. And all my own stupid fault!'

'Don't think about that now,' Kirstie said hastily. She asked Hadley if he was carrying aspirin in his saddle-bag for pain relief. He nodded, so she went over to Navaho Joe to fetch the medication and a flask of water. When she came back, Lorena May was taking in her surroundings for the first time since she regained consciousness. 'What happened to the cows?' she asked.

Kirstie handed over the aspirins. 'They're long gone. Beyond Monument Rock and down into Dead Man's Canyon, I reckon.'

'Sorry!' Lorena May sighed, pushing her hair back from her face and shivering in spite of the warm clothing pulled up around her shoulders. 'And Danny; where's he?'

Kirstie controlled a strong shudder by standing up quickly. 'We're not sure,' she answered.

'Look at me, Kirstie!' Alarm was written all over Lorena May's features in spite of Kirstie's attempt to skip over the black colt's fate. 'Something terrible happened to him, didn't it?'

She could only shake her head and turn away.

Lorena May stared around her, along the track which the escaping cattle had taken, up at the tall pines which cast a cold shadow against the rock, and then over towards the narrow strip of flat rock that formed Mountain Lion Ridge.

She saw the churned up earth where the cows had burst out of the culvert, the trampled bushes at the rim of the ledge, and then the skid marks where Danny Boy had lost his footing and slid down the steep scree slope out of sight.

'Oh!' she whispered; half groan, half sigh. She gazed up at Kirstie, her grey-green eyes wide with shock. 'Danny Boy! Oh no!'

They made the stretcher and splinted Lorena May's leg as best they could under Hadley's instructions. The next step was to ease the injured woman on to the stretcher and carry her on foot to Red Eagle Lodge.

But there were four horses to think about: Lucky and Navaho Joe, plus Silver Flash and Chigger.

Hadley thought this through and came up with the suggestion that he should lead the way with Joe while the two guests carried the stretcher. He would take them by the most direct route and meet up with the paramedics as soon as was humanly possible.

'Can you stay here with the horses until we send someone over to help you?' the old man asked Kirstie.

She nodded. 'Mom promised to round up Matt and Charlie. They'll get here quick as they can.'

'So you can handle it?' Hadley double-checked, giving Kirstie a hard stare.

'Sure!' She didn't mind being alone on the mountain. 'I want to be here!'

Hadley grunted. 'OK, but no heroics.' He glanced down at the raging river, towards the spot where Danny had vanished, refusing to leave until Kirstie had promised.

And then they left her, plodding across country towards Monument Rock. Hadley went first, a lean, stooping figure leading the Appaloosa. Lorena May lay huddled under the men's jackets, in pain but gritting her teeth. Luke and Darren carried her gently, careful not to tip or jerk the home-made stretcher.

Alone, Kirstie first made sure that the three horses in her charge were safely tethered. She checked the sky; cloud was thickening on the horizon and a wind was getting up. But it was only midday, so there was still plenty of daylight to work with. Then she made fresh radio contact with her mom, notifying her that Hadley's team had set off for the lodge and should reach it within the hour.

'Kirstie, that's great. The ambulance from San Luis got here. We're on our way up to meet

Hadley.' Sandy's voice crackled over the radio wave. 'How's Lorena May? Over.'

'She's good; cowboying up. Over.'

'OK. I got in touch with Matt and Charlie, and they're riding across to Mountain Lion Ridge. They'll be with you pretty soon. Over.'

'Thanks, Mom. Over.'

Sandy Scott signed off with the same message as Hadley. 'Hey, honey, take it easy, OK?'

Again she promised. And once more she was left with the silence of the mountain and the sight of the river rushing through the gorge below.

Danny Boy had lost his footing and slipped on a stretch of scree that sloped away at a dizzying angle. Kirstie could make out the route by following the trail of churned up earth and flattened bushes. He'd been unlucky, she realised; a couple of yards either way and the angle of the slope was less severe. The colt could have regained his balance and pulled himself back up.

Eyes narrowed to study the terrain, Kirstie crouched by the edge of the stony track, gazing down.

Along the ridge, from the culvert where he was tethered, Lucky gave a high, nervous whinny.

Kirstie stood up and walked to reassure him. 'It's OK, I'm still here. You didn't think I'd left you guys all alone!' Stroking and soothing the palomino, her gaze ranged over the steep, green sides of the culvert. 'Ain't nothing here but ground squirrels and a couple of bobcats maybe. You ain't scared of them, are you, boy?'

Lucky blew down his nostrils and stamped his foot. More settled now, he reached down to tug a mouthful of long grass from the clump at the base of a rock.

So all was quiet, and she was waiting, waiting, waiting . . .

She left the culvert and paced along the ledge, past the fatal spot; once, twice, three times. It didn't look so very steep, and there were plenty of bushes and low tree branches to grab hold of . . .

But Hadley and Sandy's warnings lingered. *No heroics. Take it easy.*

Out of sight, Lucky set up another long, high call; a signal from one horse to another that said, 'I'm here! Where are you?'

No reply from Navaho Joe, by now making his way along Miners' Ridge, halfway towards the forest ranger's lodge. The steep sides of the culvert had obviously muffled the cry.

So Lucky tried again; louder, higher, longer.

And this time a horse answered.

The cry came not from the distant rescue party, but from nearby. It was from deep in the gorge, almost lost in the rush of foaming white water; not a strong, assertive call, but weak and scared.

Kirstie stopped dead, unable to believe her ears. Was this her imagination? Or was there really a reply from down below? 'Again!' she breathed. 'Call him again!'

Lucky whinnied. *I'm here! Where are you?*

She strained to hear, hoping and praying . . .

And Danny Boy answered faintly as before. *I'm down here. Come and get me!*

No way could she resist that call.

In spite of her promises, Kirstie was going down.

But it meant using her head to work out the best route, planning ahead. There were footholds of firmer rock amongst the loose scree, and those were the spots she had to keep in her sights as she descended the slope.

On top of which, she must not look down!

Take one step at a time, grab hold of any support she could find; if she started to slip, reach out for the nearest branch, bush or tussock of grass.

Slowly, holding her breath, she proceeded.

Her boots weren't good for the job. Their soles were smooth, they had no grip. So she had to make sure to steady herself with her hands. Then it seemed best to sit for a stretch and worm her way down at a snail's pace until she reached another outcrop of solid rock.

She rested here for a while, her spine pressed flat against the slanting rock, eyes closed to shut out the plunge towards the river. But her ears let in the roar and smash of water against rock. She could smell it in all the dark, dank crevices of the cliffs below.

When at last Kirstie forced her eyes open, she realised that the outcrop of rock where she stood was a dead end as far as descending closer still to the river was concerned. She looked all ways, tried edging off the outcrop by reaching for an overhanging branch, then discovered there was nowhere for her feet to find safe purchase. She gasped and swung back. What now?

Maybe this was crazy. Had she *really* heard a horse's faint whinny from down in these dark depths, just twenty feet from where the water whirled and sped by? Could it have been her imagination, her desperation to believe that Danny Boy was still alive?

The thought made her sag and crouch, then take a deep, juddering breath.

'Kirstie!'

A wild yell from above made her look up. It was Matt, legs planted wide apart on Mountain Lion Ridge, cupping both hands around his mouth and calling at the top of his voice to make her hear. Behind him stood Charlie with a coil of rope slung across his shoulder.

'You crazy kid, what the heck d'you think you're doing?'

'Trying to save Danny Boy's life!' she cried back. The water roared in her ears and scared her to death. It smacked against rocks and the spray flew up in icy plumes. The drops hit her face like thousands of tiny, cold pin-pricks.

'Stay there. Don't move. We're coming down!' Matt made an instant decision. He and Charlie set off down the scree, their boots crunching and sliding over loose pebbles as they went. Hasty at first, they soon realised the danger of sliding out of control, so their pace slowed and they began to pick their way diagonally, zig-zagging across the scree towards Kirstie's rocky ledge.

'Lucky called and Danny answered!' she called. 'He's down here some place!'

Matt covered the final few yards then scrambled on to the rock. He peeered down at the rapids. 'No way!' he muttered, shaking his head and turning to wait for Charlie. 'Don't hold your breath,' he warned.

'Don't you believe me?' Unsure whether or not she believed it herself, Kirstie's protest was all the stronger. 'I heard him! I honestly did!'

They stood facing each other in confrontation, Matt disbelieving, Kirstie more desperate than ever.

'Hold it.' Charlie arrived with a fresh idea of what to do. 'Take a look at this rock. It forms a kind of overhang, see?'

Kirstie steeled herself to peer down over the

edge. Then she copied Charlie, who had lain full-length on his stomach and edged out to see what was under the ledge.

'Yeah, it's like Bear Hunt Overlook, only smaller!' the wrangler confirmed. A spray of river water splashed up and into his and Kirstie's faces as he spoke. 'There's maybe thirty feet of rock lengthways, going back six or eight feet into a kind of shallow cave.'

Mat too lowered himself on to his belly to join them. 'You think Danny Boy could've landed on the lower ledge?'

Charlie hesitated. 'There's a tree along there that could've broken his fall and pushed him in under the overhang,' he pointed out doubtfully.

'Yeah, so where is he now?' Matt stuck to what he regarded as the practicalities. As far as any of them could see, the area of eroded rock they were looking into was empty. He raised himself on to his knees, dismissing the theory that Charlie had offered.

But Kirstie looked again, deep under the overhang, beyond dripping tree roots, in amongst a tangle of brushwood and rotting logs which the high water had deposited in the cave. She picked up a movement, perhaps a dark shape. 'Danny?' she whispered.

There was a snap of twigs, the clip of a hoof against rock. Then a white flash; the star on the colt's forehead!

'Matt, Charlie; it's him!' Edging even further over the rim of the rock, she strained to see more.

And, hearing her voice, seeing the outline of her head and shoulders, the colt stumbled through the brushwood, his large eyes dark and liquid, his nostrils wide with fear.

'It's OK!' she promised, a break in her voice as

she took in the cuts on his legs and chest, trickling with blood, the limp on his right foreleg as he stumbled forward.

He came to a halt, body trembling, silent, gazing out of his prison-cave.

'Don't worry, Danny, we're gonna get you out!' Kirstie's heart almost broke to see him so pitiful.

'Just hold it,' Matt broke in, trying to ease Kirstie up. 'It's not as easy as you make out!'

She sprang to her feet, suddenly angry with her brother. 'What do you mean it's not easy? We found him, didn't we? Now all we have to do is get him out!'

'Matt's right.' It was Charlie's turn to try to talk sense into her. 'Freeing the horse from a situation like that is a big problem.'

'No!' she cried, putting her hands to her ears.

But Charlie was firm. He took Kirstie's hands away to make her hear. 'Danny Boy's trapped,' he insisted. 'And I don't see any way we can get him out!'

6

'We just have to think!' Kirstie's first reaction to the realisation that Danny Boy was stranded in the cave had turned into a kind of mantra that she chanted to herself while Matt and Charlie persuaded her to climb back up to the trail.

'We must think . . . we must think! Somehow we have to get him out!'

For what were the only other options? Two, as far as she could make out.

One would be to abandon Danny there on the ledge, where, if the mountain lions didn't get him, then a combination of starvation and the freezing night-time temperatures surely would.

The second was a choice that Matt had already mentioned to Charlie in a low voice, hoping that Kirstie wouldn't overhear. 'It'd be kinder to the little guy if I came back with my gun tomorrow morning and put him out of his misery.'

They'd looked at the situation every which way, trying to judge whether they could use ropes to haul Danny Boy off the ledge, and decided no, it wouldn't work because of the overhang. Then maybe they could fix slings under his belly and lower him into the water? Again, no. Even if the colt would tolerate being hoisted over the river, what then? The current was so fierce that lowering him into it would mean certain death.

And all the time Charlie and Matt had talked on the rock, Kirstie had been trying to soothe and reassure the trapped horse.

Danny Boy had inched to the outer edge of his ledge, craning his neck upwards, trying in vain to reach her outstretched hand. His black mane hung limply over his face and neck, dripping with dirty water that splashed down from the roof of the cave. The gashes from the fall gaped red and ugly.

'He needs a tetanus shot!' Kirstie had insisted to her veterinary student brother. 'Those cuts look nasty. And if he has to stay here overnight, while we figure out a way of rescuing him, he needs food and water!'

Matt had shrugged and turned away, indicating that treating and feeding the horse could be a waste of time.

But Kirstie had refused to leave the rock until Matt would at least promise to hold off from, as he put it, 'putting Danny out of his misery'. He'd agreed at least that Kirstie could return with hay and clean water before it grew dark, which would give them the evening to talk things through with Sandy.

Even so, it had just about torn her apart to leave Danny Boy there.

'I know you can't understand what's happening,' she'd whispered. 'You only know you're trapped in there and that soon it's gonna get cold and dark. So, sure you're scared that a cougar will come along, or bears. Then what will you do?

'I'm scared too. But, Danny, I'll be back with food before nightfall. Then you'll see that we haven't abandoned you. You gotta be patient. Give us some time to work this thing out.'

'Kirstie!' Charlie had been the one to finally raise her from the overhang. 'Time to go.'

And that had been the dreadful wrench; Danny Boy whinnying for her to stay, Charlie and Matt leading her up the scree, hearing him call after her all the while they rode by Monument Rock, along Miners' Ridge, until finally his cry faded as they dropped into Dead Man's Canyon and headed for home.

She kept her promise and returned with Charlie, once more negotiating the dangerous scree slope from ridge to overhang; this time with hay-flaps stuffed into rucksacks which they strapped to their backs. Charlie also carried a container of fresh water, with the plan of fixing a rope to a tree branch and abseiling down into the cave to drop off the vital supplies.

Back at the ranch, meanwhile, Sandy was supervising the sending of Lorena May to hospital in San Luis, having successfully met up with Hadley's rescue team as planned.

Dusk was falling and the snow clouds sweeping

in as Kirstie and Charlie made it back to Mountain Lion Ridge with the feed. It gave them very little time to climb safely down and back again. But they found, as before, that hurrying down the scree was impossible. It took care and caution to pick out the route, driven on by Danny's faint whinny from below.

They made it at last, with light snowflakes drifting down from the leaden sky.

Kirstie unpacked the hay-flaps while Charlie slung his rope over a branch at the near end of the ledge, handing them to him after he'd secured the end of the rope around his waist. He lowered himself down the sheer drop for ten or so feet, relying on the strength of the rope, finding footholds, until he reached Danny's ledge. Then he crouched under the shallow entrance to the cave and crawled along to drop off the hay.

And all this while, Danny Boy waited, sensing that the rope and the wrangler were here to help, coming eagerly forward to eat and drink, despite his sore leg.

Watching from above, Kirstie was satisfied. Now, at least, Danny wouldn't starve.

But they had to get back to the horses and ride

the trail as fast as they could to reach home again before the true, pitch-black darkness of a moonless night blanketed the mountains. They rode hard, without speaking, until the yellow lights of the ranch house glittered in the valley below. Then Kirstie allowed herself to slacken off. She reined Lucky from a lope to a trot, knowing that they'd done all they could for today.

'Thanks, Charlie,' she murmured, glancing sideways to see his face hidden under the shade of his hat as he rode Rodeo Rocky back into the corral. 'Tomorrow we think of a way to get Danny out, huh?'

'Sure,' he replied. His voice sounded hollow in the empty yard. He repeated it: 'Sure we do.'

So why didn't she believe him as she unsaddled Lucky, fed him and led him out into the dark meadow?

Kirstie's mom and brother were huddled over a map spread out on the kitchen table when she finally made it into the ranch house.

'Mom had an idea that maybe we could reach Danny Boy by river,' Matt explained, glancing up at her exhausted face. 'But honest to God, Kirstie,

I don't see how we get a boat down these rapids. And even if we could, how would we persuade an injured horse to jump from a ledge into a boat or even on to a raft?'

She nodded without speaking, watching Sandy sigh and fold away the map.

'We had a message from the hospital,' Matt went on. 'The doctors diagnosed a mild concussion. And Hadley got it right, as usual; Lorena broke her leg in two places.'

'But she'll be OK?' At least one aspect of the day's disaster was working out.

'Yeah, fine.' Matt watched Kirstie carefully as Sandy brought her supper. 'I spoke to her. She said she's real sorry for what she did, and no way was Hadley or anyone from the ranch to blame.'

'So at least she won't try to sue us!' Kirstie gave a tired smile.

'No, and don't even joke about it!' Sandy sighed. 'An accident would have to happen during the one week we have a ranch full of vacation organisers. I only hope the message gets through to them that Lorena takes full responsibility for what happened.'

'Darren and Luke were both there.' Kirstie

relived the moment when Luke had driven the final cow out of the culvert, right into Danny Boy's path. 'They'll tell everyone.'

'Yeah, I hope.' Wearily, Sandy sat at the table. The lamp on the windowsill cast light on her fair hair but left her face in shadow. 'So what do we do about Danny?'

Kirstie felt Matt brace himself to deliver what he knew would be an unpopular verdict. 'My feeling is, it's pretty hopeless out there—' he began.

'No, it's not!' Fear darted deep into Kirstie and made her cry out in protest. She pushed away her plate and stood up. 'Danny didn't get badly hurt in the fall; only a few cuts and a small limp. What's hopeless about that?'

'Hush, honey.' Sandy reached out her hand to steady her. 'We have to listen to what Matt has to say.'

'Firstly, there's the fact that, come night-time, it's way below zero. That's why Jim was so keen for us to help with the round-up; he knew his cattle wouldn't make it through too many more nights. And a horse hates the cold worse than anything. So it ain't fair to leave Danny longer than we have to.'

Kirstie's eyes blazed. 'I know it! Don't think I *want* him to be out there!'

'Matt never said you did,' Sandy said quietly. 'Let him go on.'

'Second, what happens if a mountain lion gets into that cave with him? Danny wouldn't stand a chance!'

Shutting her eyes tight, this time Kirstie had no reply. Yes, it was cougar country out there beyond Monument Rock. The very name of the ridge told you that. It was a wild landscape with plenty of bush cover and exactly the kind of rocky outcrop that the lions liked. In her imagination, she caught a glimpse of a sandy-coloured coat, huge paws with long talons, a flash of white fangs . . .

Sandy frowned. 'It sounds harsh, but maybe you're right, Matt.'

Again panic overtook Kirstie's sense of reason. 'He's not!' she cried. 'Mom, all we have to do is think some more!'

'And then what?' Matt argued. He stood with his back to the light, his tall frame outlined against the dark window.

'If I knew the answer to that, then we wouldn't still have to be thinking!'

'Kirstie, honey...'

'No!' Shaking her head, Kirstie ran to the bottom of the stairs. 'I don't know how Matt can even be thinking what he's thinking! Who's gonna do it, Matt? Are *you* gonna take a gun, aim and fire at Danny Boy with your own hands?'

She stopped, hardly able to breathe, her voice choked with emotion as she delivered her final sentence before dashing upstairs. 'Because if you do, believe me, I'll never *ever* speak to you again!'

A broken night inhabited by ghostly mountain lions and giant snowdrifts that broke the boundary between sleep and waking was the price Kirstie paid for arguing with Matt. She tossed and turned, pulled the blankets over her head, emerged pale and tousled with no appetite for the breakfast her mom laid before her.

'It snowed,' Sandy said quietly. 'But not much. And the forecast for today is good.'

'Hmm.' Leaning on her elbows, Kirstie paid little attention.

'The weather won't stop the rides, at least.'

'Yeah, good.'

'Lisa called to say she'd stop by for a visit.'

Rubbing her tired eyes, Kirstie nodded. 'Did you tell her about Danny Boy?'

'She already knew. Smiley Gilpin drove over from Red Eagle Lodge to Lisa's grandpa's place and told him the news. Lennie spoke to Bonnie on the phone, and Bonnie told Lisa.' Word, as usual, had got round fast.

'So, what did you say?' Clenching her fists to absorb her mom's overnight decision on Danny's fate, Kirstie stared at the table.

'I told Lisa both yours and Matt's point of view, and that though I'd slept on it, I still hadn't quite made up my mind . . .'

'Mom, please!' She turned in her chair. 'We can't shoot Danny!'

'I know. I hear you. But what if keeping him alive just prolongs his suffering, as Matt says?' Sandy seemed almost as wretched as Kirstie as she tried to come to a decision. 'I said this to Bonnie after Lisa had come off the phone. It was Bonnie who said not to rush into anything.'

'Yes, right!' *Exactly!* What Kirstie needed was just a little more time!

'According to Bonnie, Lisa may have had an idea about getting Danny out.' Doubtful and anxious not to raise her daughter's hopes too far, still Sandy wanted to put her in the picture.

'She did? What idea?' Kirstie was up on her feet, ready to drag the information from Sandy if necessary.

'Bonnie didn't say. But that's the reason Lisa wants to pay us a visit; to discuss this possibility . . .'

'And what did you say?'

'I said, sure, we needed all the help we could get.'

'So that means you won't let Matt go out there and . . . and do what he wants to do?' Kirstie's grey eyes bored into Sandy's face, searching for the answer she wanted to hear.

'Not yet,' Sandy agreed at last. 'No guns. Not until we've heard what Lisa has to say.'

Kirstie waited at her bedroom window for her friend to arrive. Would it be Bonnie's car or Lennie Goodman's pick-up that drove under the timber entrance where the sign with the words 'Half-Moon Ranch' swung in the wind?

Down in the corral she could see Ben, Charlie and Matt busy with the morning routine of brushing and saddling the horses, with Hadley wandering down from Brown Bear Cabin to lend a hand with the raking.

A bunch of guests, including Darren and Luke, had gathered outside the tack-room, huddled together with their jacket collars turned up, obviously discussing Lorena May's accident and its aftermath.

'C'mon, Lisa!' Kirstie muttered to herself for the hundredth time. The minutes seemed to drag, and still the road winding out of sight through the forest was quiet.

Then, at nine-thirty, after Matt and the two wranglers had led their groups off along the trail, Lennie's pick-up appeared.

Kirstie spotted its trail of dust along the road, waited until she could be sure, then raced downstairs into the yard in time to see Lisa leap out and run towards her.

'Hey!' Lisa swerved around Hadley, who was walking between the tack-room and the house. She brandished what looked like a sheet of neatly folded, yellowish-white paper. 'I got here as quick as I could!'

'Lisa, do I need to talk with you!' Kirstie sighed,

pulling her on to the porch out of the wind. 'What's this idea you have about Danny?'

'It's all in here!' She pointed to the paper, her eyes bright, then began to unfold it and spread it flat on the seat of the porch swing.

'What is? What have you got there?' Kirstie made out a hand-drawn map whose edges were worn and whose creases were torn. At first sight she felt her heart sink. How on earth could this help them to rescue Danny?

'You see this? It's a map of the old silver mining area along Big Bear River. I knew Grandpa kept it in his bureau. When I was a little kid, he used to take it out and tell me stories about the guys who worked the mines—'

'Like Miner John?' Kirstie cut in, glancing up at Hadley and Lennie locked in conversation by the pick-up.

Lisa's grandpa was a small, slight man of almost seventy who still ran the Lone Elm Trailer Park over the ridge from Half-Moon Ranch.

'Yeah, right; Miner John! Exactly Miner John!' In her excitement, Lisa almost let the map fly away. But she darted forward and pinned it back down. 'Here's the river, see! Now these crosses marked on the bank indicate claims made by the miners between 1856 and 1902, and these dotted lines show how far they tunnelled into the hillside using dynamite to carve out a passage.'

Kirstie leaned over Lisa's shoulder and nodded. 'But what does this have to do with Danny Boy?'

'I'm coming to that. Listen, when I heard about the accident on Mountain Lion Ridge, and how the colt was trapped, I got to thinking about Grandpa's old map. I said to myself, what if some of these old tunnels are still open? And again, what if one of them were to come out close to where Danny is stuck?'

'Yes!' Now she understood! It was like striking a seam of silver; the feeling of discovery and joy! 'So where's the ridge on this map?' she demanded.

'Here.' Lisa pointed. 'See, "Mountain Lion Ridge". Look, dotted lines telling you there are underground passages.'

Kirstie bit her lip and nodded.

'The problem is, there are so many. So I talked with grandpa. He says that it's even worse than it looks. Not all the claims and tunnels appear on the map, and the mountainside around there is riddled with as many holes as—'

'—Swiss cheese!' Kirstie said rapidly. 'Yeah, that's what Hadley says too. And you know, the most famous claim of all – Miner John's – can't possibly be marked because no one ever found out where it was!'

'Right!' Lisa could see that Kirstie's thoughts had finally caught up with hers. 'It's gonna be difficult, but you see what I'm getting at?'

'Yeah. I've been looking at this whole thing from the wrong angle!' Kirstie admitted. 'I've been racking my brains trying to find a way to get Danny off that ledge and up the scree slope the same way he fell. But that's no good. What I should have been doing is working out where that cave at the back of the ledge leads to!'

Lisa nodded and tapped the map. 'My bet is, it'll link up with the old silver mine workings. And who knows; maybe even with the secret entrance used by Miner John himself!'

7

It wasn't easy to persuade Sandy Scott to let Kirstie and Lisa loose on the mountain armed with an old map, a rope and a couple of head torches.

At first she simply shook her head and said, 'No way.'

'Why not?' To Kirstie it was crystal clear: exploring the disused mine shafts was the only, and she meant *the only*, way of saving Danny.

'It's obvious why not, honey.' Sandy tried to be kind but firm. 'The silver mines along Mountain

Lion Ridge have been closed down for fifty years or more. No one goes in there to maintain them.'

'Yeah, but what difference does that make?' Lisa backed Kirstie up strongly. She'd arrived at the ranch dressed in old jeans and a waterproof jacket, ready for action, her thick, wavy red hair neatly tucked away under a black baseball cap. 'A tunnel's a tunnel. Period. So what if no one's been down there for years?'

'For starters, you can get a roof fall, any time, any place.' Sandy tried to stay calm in the face of the girls' demands. 'Second, those shafts flood each time the water level in Big Bear River rises. Anyone who enters the tunnels is taking a mighty big risk.'

'Yes, but it's no bigger risk than the miners used to take every day of their lives!' Kirstie argued. Frown lines marked her forehead; her grey eyes grew fiercely stubborn. This was one argument she just had to win.

'And look how many of them ended up in shallow graves under Monument Rock!' Sandy pointed out.

'But think of Danny Boy!' Kirstie pleaded. 'He's already been trapped out there for one night. We have to help him, Mom!'

Shaking her head and sighing, Sandy took Lisa and Kirstie down into the yard to confer with the two old men by the pick-up. Once more she expressed her strong doubts.

'It's sure true, there's danger in it,' Lennie conceded. 'But I recall way back, when Hadley and me were kids, boys would take on a dare to go down the shafts. I went down myself, many times. Foolish maybe, but I guess we even thought we might strike it rich one day!'

'You see!' Kirstie insisted. 'Hadley and Lennie didn't come to any harm!'

'But that was – how many years ago? Fifty or sixty!' Head to one side, Sandy was visibly weakening. 'Did you come across rock-falls?' she quizzed.

Lennie shrugged. 'Not new ones. Most of the shafts are shored up by mighty strong props. It's only the ones that failed to produce much silver that caved in because they dug 'em fast and pretty soon abandoned 'em.'

'So you really think it's possible to go in higher up the mountain and discover a way leading out on to the river?'

'Sure.' Hadley explained the system. 'The river was where the miners panned for silver. They'd heave a load of rock out from under the mountain and cart it down along an underground railway line to the nearest exit on to Big Bear River. The rock was tipped into one of those boxes you can still see beside the sluices. Then you had a hydraulic pump lifting water out of the river to wash away the dirt and loose rock.'

'And, eureka!' Lennie added. 'The ore stayed in the bottom of the box, and that was your meal ticket out of there to the gin palaces, saloons and dance halls of the big city!'

Sandy considered what she'd heard. 'Put like that, it sounds like a pretty organised system.'

Behind her back, Kirstie showed her crossed fingers to Lisa. But she kept quiet; now was not the time to put on more pressure.

'I'll tell you what,' Lennie offered. 'This colt is important to Kirstie; anyone can see that.'

'She worked real hard with him,' Lisa reminded them. 'They said he was a hard horse to handle, that he'd never make it as a ranch horse, but Kirstie was the one who proved them wrong!'

A lump formed in Kirstie's throat as she ducked

her head and stared at her boots. Her fingers were still tightly crossed behind her back.

Lennie nodded. 'So how would it be if me and Hadley took charge here? I mean, us old guys don't have anything too pressing to do with our time, and we sure have the know-how to oversee whatever it is the girls want to do.'

Something seemed to click in Sandy's head and her troubled face cleared a little. 'And you wouldn't let them do anything too risky?' she checked.

'No, ma'am. My idea would be for Kirstie and Lisa to ride up the Ridge with Hadley with feed for the horse. Then they could scout around up by Monument Rock. Meanwhile, I plan to take a drive into Mineville.'

'To do what?' A still thoughtful Sandy glanced at Kirstie's eager face.

'I want to call in on Gus McDonald in the museum. He holds some pretty detailed site plans of the old mines which could prove helpful once we get this search underway.'

'Great idea!' Lisa cried.

Kirstie said nothing, but she felt she could have kissed and hugged the sweet little old man with his silver-rimmed glasses and shiny, twinkling face.

'OK!' Sandy said finally, to a flood of relief. 'Let's give it a try. But on one important condition . . .'

'Which is?' Kirstie knew that the limit was going to be a tough one from which her mom would never shift.

'That we do it your way for twenty four hours maximum. After that, I'll have to do it Matt's way.'

Kirstie swallowed hard and managed not to protest. She knew the reason; that to go on for longer without success would only prolong Danny Boy's misery.

The deadline was reasonable, and in a way made her even more determined. 'We'll do it!' she swore, as much to herself as to the small knot of people standing in the yard.

Then she broke away and went to saddle Lucky. There wasn't a moment to lose.

They heard Danny crying out from the cave when they were way up the mountain.

'He's alive!' Lisa whispered, keeping Jitterbug moving at a fast trot along Miners' Ridge. The dainty sorrel horse was fresh and eager, her ears pricked in the direction of Danny Boy's call.

'Yeah, but scared.' Kirstie could hear it in the high, repetitive whinny. 'It's terrible for a horse to be out alone and trapped. He's a herd animal. He needs other horses around him for protection.'

'It takes a tough horse to make it through Danny's situation,' Hadley agreed. 'I know plenty who would just lay down and die.'

But not Danny! Kirstie was determined to reach him and convince the colt yet again that he hadn't been forgotten. She was glad when Lucky took in the message from the trapped horse and answered him at regular intervals as they passed Bear Hunt Overlook and drew nearer to the scene of the accident.

On any other day, the riders under Monument Rock would have stopped to take in the breathtaking beauty of the scene. The tall pines were sprinkled with snow, the borders of the creeks frosted over with clear ice which tinkled as it broke away. Blue jays broke from the cover of overhead branches, a flash of vivid colour against the white slopes, while pikas and chipmunks scurried along logs. The small furry creatures bleated and chattered their warnings about the approaching horses and riders to the hidden bobcats and stealthy coyotes.

But Kirstie and Lisa had no eyes for the creatures of the mountains. They talked little, rode hard. Close behind, Hadley took note of the direction of the wind and cloud conformation; signals of the type of weather building up for later in the day.

It was Lisa's first view of the scene of Lorena May's accident, so she asked many questions as Kirstie went through the same routine as before of approaching Danny's cave with hay and water.

'How come this Lorena May person didn't realise she was in the way of the cattle?' she wanted to know, shocked by the length of Danny's fall and scared by the force of the water tumbling through the canyon below.

'Too busy taking snapshots, I guess.' Kirstie recalled bitterly the visitor's eagerness to capture the perfect Kodak moment. Anyhow, it was done, and the job was to get down to the ledge and make Danny comfortable before they scouted higher up the hill with Hadley.

Today Kirstie was the one to sling a rope over the tree branch and abseil down to the colt's level with hay and water. She could hear him snorting and stamping, prepared herself for his wild, weary appearance when she finally stepped on to the ledge.

But even so, she hadn't expected him to look as he did – hunted, cornered, almost defeated.

'Danny!' she murmured, standing quite still.

His head was up high in fear, his eyes staring. Tense, ready to rear and strike her with his hooves if she approached, the black colt seemed not even to recognise her.

'It's me,' she whispered, making her voice sound calm and gentle, though she too was afraid. 'You had a bad night, huh? I know, it's hard. But I brought you something to eat, see?'

Gradually Danny Boy seemed to relax. His head came down and reached forward to the food she was offering.

'Yeah; easy, boy.' Kirstie took a step forward, knowing that her fear, if she showed it, would instantly transmit to the horse. So she ignored the spookiness of the dank place, the icy drips from above and the slimy puddles under her feet.

She offered a fistful of alfalfa, waiting for him to approach in his own time.

'How's it going down there?' Lisa's anxious voice broke the silence. She'd stayed by the tree where they'd secured the rope, out of sight above the overhang.

Danny Boy started and half-reared. His hooves came down with a clash on the rock less than a yard from where Kirstie stood.

She didn't flinch. 'We're doing good,' she called back to Lisa. 'Yeah, we are, aren't we, Danny? It's me, Kirstie. Don't you know me? So who scared you? Was it some enemy who came to your cave during the night? Or was it nightmares inside your own head?'

All the time she talked, she was checking the colt for signs of more cuts; the slash of talons, the bite of knife-sharp teeth. But no, there was nothing to show that he'd been in a fight, thank goodness. It seemed that no predator had cornered him in his dark, lonely cave, and that Danny Boy alone had worked himself into this state of dread.

But now he was coming to his senses, and the need for food was overcoming his fright. He approached, head still down, eyes rolling, the white flash on his face gleaming eerily.

At last he edged near enough to stretch out for the hay. Kirstie felt his lips snatch the food from the palm of her hand. Then she was able to move in with more, close enough to begin to stroke his neck and gently rub his shoulders, passing her hands lightly over his quivering body. She soothed him as he ate, moving quietly to unbuckle his cinch and remove the saddle with its broken stirrup leather. Probably the dragging stirrup had been one of the things that had spooked him so badly. Then she decided to loosen the noseband on the colt's bosal, but not to take it right off. Ben's special bridle would be needed if it came to leading Danny out of here.

Not 'if', but 'when', she corrected herself. '*When* we lead you out of here!'

She'd done all she could, so she left him on a confident note, determined not to cast a backwards glance that might dent that optimism. Quickly she took hold of the rope and hauled herself up to the tree. Breathless, she nodded to Lisa, who unhitched the noose, and together the girls climbed back to the ridge.

Even with a map, Kirstie felt that they were in a needle in a haystack situation.

The area they were exploring covered roughly a square mile, bounded by the river below and Monument Rock above, with Bear Hunt Overlook as the southern limit and Eagle's Peak itself to the north.

'It's more like a honeycomb than Swiss cheese!' Kirstie muttered after Lisa had pulled out the folded sheet and spread it on a flat rock. The more closely they studied it, the more crosses they found, each one indicating a claim made by the old miners.

In places the map was worn away, in others, wet fingers had smudged the old-fashioned lettering, making it difficult to keep their bearings.

Luckily, Hadley knew the territory so well that he could fill in the gaps. 'This here is Monument Rock.' He stabbed at the map with a calloused, broken-nailed finger. 'We're standing right here, at the southern end of Mountain Lion Ridge.'

'So if all the crosses on the slope show entrances to mine shafts, what we have to do is follow the broken lines until they meet up with one of the old sluice boxes.' Lisa squinted at the map as if she was near sighted.

'Because the broken lines are tunnels,' Kirstie murmured to herself. 'And what we need is one coming out on to Danny's ledge, which is marked right here.' She pointed to a spot which she thought must be correct, according to the bends in the river and the position in relation to Monument Rock. But she looked to the old wrangler for confirmation.

'Right,' he agreed. He gazed down the slope to the river, then nodded again. 'That sluice box on the promontory right under Danny's ledge is marked sure enough.'

'But no dotted line leading to it.' The tip of Lisa's nose was practically glued to the map. 'That's weird, ain't it?'

'Unless the sluice belonged to one of those claims that was never registered,' Kirstie suggested. She followed Hadley's line of vision to pick out the broken-down chute on crumbling wooden stilts that stuck out from a spur of rock fifeen or twenty feet into the whirling current. 'In which case, they may have dynamited into the rock and linked up with one of the tunnels that *does* appear on the map. So what we should do, is find the nearest one that's marked, locate the entrance up by Monument Rock, go down it and hope to find a tunnel branching off when we get down to river level. With luck, that's the shaft that will lead out on to Danny's ledge!'

When Kirstie had been through all this, Lisa gave a short laugh. 'Dead simple . . . Not!'

'Well, *I* know what I mean!' Kirstie's nervousness made her jumpy. The cold wind swept along Mountain Lion Ridge from the north, rustling dry leaves out of hollows and raising the thin covering of powdery snow. 'And I reckon it'll work!'

'Yeah, but I reckon we need that site plan from Gus McDonald. It's gonna give us much more detailed information.' Lisa looked at her watch to judge how much longer it would be before her grandpa reached them. 'Maybe we just ought to wait until it arrives.'

'And lose a couple of hours?' Kirstie shook her head, taking the map and folding it neatly. 'This is good enough to be going on with.' She turned to Hadley. 'Will the horses make it up to

Monument Rock, or do we leave them tethered here on the ridge?'

'Leave them here,' he decided. 'We can put them in the culvert, out of the wind. They can rest up while we climb on foot.'

'And what about the weather?' Now that it came to the point of scouting around and choosing an entrance to an old shaft, Lisa's nerve was beginning to give way. 'Hey, Hadley; what's gonna happen with the clouds over the Peak?'

The old man shrugged, automatically tugging at his jacket collar to shield his neck from the cold.

'No one said the forecast was bad, did they?' Kirstie pointed out. 'Listen, are we gonna do this, or not?'

Lisa gritted her teeth. 'We are!'

'So let's fetch the head torches and ropes from the saddle-bags and get on up there!' Kirstie was all thumbs as she tied Lucky's lead-rope to an aspen in the culvert, then rummaged in the bag for the equipment they would need.

Ready before Lisa and Hadley, she cut off from

114

the trail and began the climb towards Monument Rock.

'Site plans . . . weather!' she grumbled under her breath. 'Waiting for two whole hours. No way!'

What did weather or anything else have to do with it when Danny's life was at stake?

8

Five rough headstones marked the last resting place of miners who had lost the race for silver in the Eldorado days of the late eighteen hundreds. Their moss-covered graves lay in the deep shadow of Monument Rock. Crudely chiselled letters gave little more than than their names and the dates they died.

'Frank Chisum, d.1878', 'Red Wolcott, 1893. R.I.P.', 'S. McSween, shot dead by Alfred E. Noon, 1882.'

'Uhh!' Lisa read the nearest stones, then

shuddered as she and Kirstie climbed on up the hill ahead of the old ranch hand. 'I wonder if they ever caught Alfred!'

'Can't you just picture it?' Kirstie breathed. Lean men with heavy moustaches, worn down by backbreaking work, most likely squabbling over a foot or two of land that they believed would hold the hidden solution to all their troubles. The long six-shooters, the bullets bouncing off the rocks, embedding themselves into the trunks of the ancient pine trees. The one fatal shot that had ended the life of poor S. McSween.

'Sure!' Lisa paused to wait for Hadley. 'It's kinda spooky up here,' she admitted.

While they waited, Kirstie pulled out the map and began to identify the places where mine shafts ought to be. 'There's one marked this side of Monument Rock,' she pointed out, 'and two more a couple of hundred yards the other side. But all three tunnels come out by the river, a good half mile from where we need to be.'

'So, that's no good.' As Kirstie studied the map, Lisa was poking around for signs of the actual entrances to the old mines. She came across one that began as a natural crevice in pinkish-grey granite rock then developed after a few feet into a man-made tunnel. Trees disguised the mouth of the shaft, and over the years many animals had made their dens. There was a dank smell, piles of brushwood, even small bones and scraps of fur to show that a coyote or a bobcat had once dined well.

Lisa emerged, wrinkling her nose. 'How are we gonna choose which shaft to explore?' she asked Kirstie. 'And how are we gonna mark our way? Because I sure as anything don't want to get lost down there!'

Kirstie agreed. 'That's why I'm crossing out the shafts which give us no chance of ending up close to Danny's ledge,' she explained. 'I'm already down to two possibles ... wait ...' She traced another dotted line down to the river, then gave an exasperated sigh. 'No, make that one. We're down to one possible.'

As she followed the last route with her finger, Hadley came up to discuss the situation. From the high vantage point, breathing hard, he looked down into the valley and slowly gave his opinion. 'My feeling is, you ain't gonna find the shaft you want on any map.'

'Don't say that!' Still believing in their plan, Kirstie traced the final option, only to find that this tunnel ended three hundred yards downstream from where they wanted to be. She sighed and slumped over the map.

But Hadley wasn't deterred. 'I got a distinct memory that promontory with the old, unmarked sluice box is the one we picked out when we were kids as being Miner John's claim.'

'Hey!' Lisa brightened at this. Like every kid for miles around, she'd been told the legend of the secretive miner. And, like every kid, she'd dreamed of coming up to Monument Rock to discover the hoard of long-forgotten silver in John's hidden mine.

'Are you sure?' Kirstie asked.

'Not a hundred per cent,' he admitted. 'We're talking a long time back. But if I'm right, it was passed down by word of mouth since my grandpa's time that this was the place where John panned for silver. The only problem was, us kids could never get at the sluice to find out more.'

'And did you look for the entrance up here by the rock?'

'I guess.' Hadley's memory wasn't so clear on

119

this. 'We rode hereabouts, but none of us much liked the place because of the graves. There was stuff about ghosts; you know how kids are!'

'Yeah!' Lisa pulled her jacket closer around her neck and glanced up at the branches whipped back and forth by the wind.

'OK!' Kirstie took stock. She pointed to the bend in the river where the old sluice jutted out from the promontory beneath Danny's ledge. 'We think that's Miner John's site. We also think there's a secret entrance up here by the Rock.'

'A *very* secret entrance!' Lisa reminded her that it had remained hidden for more than a hundred years.

Kirstie nodded. 'But it's an entrance big enough to get a mule through, because John took his silver into town on Jethro, right? And a mule with panniers isn't small.' Striding away from the headstones towards the tall pillar of rock as she figured things out, she scoured every crevice and hidden corner.

Lisa and Hadley joined in, snapping thin branches to reveal damp hollows, brushing away layers of powdery snow, bending under shallow overhangs and always eventually stepping back in disappointment.

After half an hour of searching, Hadley reacted to a signal on his radio by pulling the receiver from his pocket. His cold hands fumbled with the controls.

'Lennie to Hadley. Over.'

'Yeah, Lennie. Go ahead. Over.'

Lisa and Kirstie drew near to listen.

'Hadley, bad news down here. I'm in Mineville and it's snowing pretty bad. What's it like up there? Over.'

'Snow on the way,' Hadley reported. 'But it ain't here yet. We got two, maybe three hours before it sets in. Over.'

'So how're y'all doing? Over.'

'No luck so far, Lennie. I'm thinking maybe we should postpone our activities on account of the snow. Over.'

'No!' Kirstie sprang back and made a big show of continuing to search. Twenty four hours was all they had, and if they went away now and the snow blocked their return, then all would be lost. So she went right up to the rock and jumped on to a ledge two feet from the ground, turning around to get the best vantage point.

'Watch out, Kirstie!' Lisa warned. 'There's ice on those high rocks!'

'. . . OK, Lennie, I'll call the ranch, find out what Sandy wants us to do. Over!' Hadley switched off the radio and stood thoughtfully looking up at Kirstie.

'There's an entrance here somewhere!' she muttered, edging along the narrow, backwards-sloping ledge.

Glancing up, she glimpsed the swift clouds and the tall chimney of rock towering over her. Below were the miners' graves, and beyond them, felled timber and half uprooted trees clinging to the steep slope all the way down to the curving river.

Dizzy at the sight and realising that her ledge sloped away at an angle of forty five degrees down into a hidden, shallow cave, Kirstie reached out for a handhold, overbalanced and slid backwards on the ice. Her arms flailed, but her feet slipped from under her and she went down hard, first on to her knees and then on to her belly.

It was like going down a slide feet-first, grappling at the icy surface with her outstretched fingers as the world disappeared from view.

Seconds later, she came to a sudden halt as her feet hit something hollow. Not rock. Wood. That was right; a wooden barrier had stopped her from being swallowed up by the giant jaws of Monument Rock.

'You OK?' Lisa yelled. 'I can't see you. Can you answer me?'

'Yeah, I'm in here!' Kirstie called back from her pit. 'Listen, I need to put on my head torch . . . that's better. I think there's a door down here . . .'

'Kirstie!' Scrambling on to the ledge, Lisa made her way along on hands and knees. She peered down into the gloom, picking out the yellow beam of Kirstie's torch.

'. . . It is; it's a door! Oh, yuck, there's so much dirt! Wait . . .'

'I'm coming down!' Lisa cried. And she launched herself feet first down the slope.

She landed next to Kirstie, bundling into her and knocking her sideways.

'See?' Kirstie recovered quickly. Her fingertips explored the rotting wood, searching for a primitive latch that would open the door into whatever lay beyond. 'Brackets!' she whispered as she made contact with the rusting metal and the dim light fell on them.

Then Lisa gasped her name. She pointed to a spot in the centre of the door. 'Lucky horseshoe!'

Kirstie held her breath as she lifted the iron shoe from its ancient nail. She felt its chilly surface, roughened by decades of rust, then she held it up into the lamp's beam. 'Lisa, this isn't a horseshoe,' she whispered, her eyes gleaming. She felt the weight, judged the size and shape. 'This shoe belonged to a mule!'

'Before you set foot beyond that door, you gotta promise that you'll check back with me every fifteen minutes!' Hadley was clear as could be on the ground rules. The decision had already been made that he would stay at the tunnel entrance to keep in touch with Sandy Scott, giving her a regular report on the girls' progress. But before they set off, he drilled them strictly.

'Two, you gotta carry ropes and wear your lamps at all times. Three, if there's a problem with the roof of the tunnel, you turn right around and come back, OK?'

Fiddling with the strap on her head torch,

Kirstie nodded. Her whole body was strung out like a tight wire. 'Gee!' she said over and over, whenever the realisation hit her that she'd literally stumbled across Miner John's shaft.

'Thank you, Jethro!' she'd cried, as she and Lisa had scrambled back to the surface. She'd held up the mule's iron shoe for Hadley to see; the concrete proof they needed that she'd hit upon the right shaft.

There'd been no more talk then of being overtaken by the weather and forced back to the ranch. Hadley had agreed that their luck was in and that they must give it one big shot.

And now she and Lisa were ready. Her heart was thumping, her mouth was dry.

'OK, Danny; we're on our way!' she muttered, climbing on to the ledge and taking a last glance down into the valley.

As if in telepathic response, Lucky set up a chain of whinnies from his sheltered spot in the culvert. He gave the call which announced his presence, passed it on to Jitterbug, who passed it on to Silver Flash. Then there was a pause, as if the three horses were waiting. Kirstie, Lisa and Hadley listened hard.

Seconds later came a thin, high neigh. *I'm here. Come and get me!*

'Danny Boy!' Kirstie murmured. Then she and Lisa eased their way down the icy slope to Miner John's door.

''Course it had to be locked!' Lisa grunted. She'd shoved with her shoulder and the door hadn't budged.

'Bolted from the inside,' Kirstie guessed. 'That figures.' Maybe it was more than a century since anyone had last trodden this path, but if you thought it through, no way would Miner John have left his precious seam of silver unguarded. And if he'd been unexpectedly swept to his death in the icy river, it followed that the bolts on the door would have stayed locked forever.

Lisa was about to turn and yell to Hadley for help, but Kirstie stopped her.

'It's no problem,' she pointed out. 'Some of these planks are so rotten I can tear them away with my bare hands.'

As soon as she'd removed three of the strips of wood, the gap was wide enough for them to squeeze through.

'Remember, check back with me in fifteen minutes!' Hadley called from above, his voice already fading.

'We're in!' Lisa took a deep breath then blew out noisily through her cheeks. When she tried to stand up straight, she hit her head on the roof of the tunnel, ducked again and stumbled against the side. 'Ouch! . . . Ugh!'

'What is it?' Kirstie peered into total darkness. Her lamp made a feeble impression on the rough rock walls carved out by dynamite and pick.

'Slime!' Lisa shuddered and wiped her hands on her jeans. 'Oh, and yuck, cobwebs!'

'Don't think about it!' Kirstie hissed. *Spiders, small scuttling things, flitting things, creeping, crawling, rustling things . . .*

Concentrate! Put one foot after the other, follow the downward slope of Miner John's shaft.

'Maybe we'll find silver!' Lisa made a feeble attempt to lighten the mood.

'Aagh!' Kirstie had walked into something which felt like a squid's tentacle grabbing at her face and shoulder. When she turned her lamp on it, she saw that it was a long, twisted tree root which had made its way through cracks in the rock down from the surface. Underfoot, her boots splashed through water; probably snow melt. The sound echoed and made a small trickle sound like a running creek.

'Hey, look; a pick and a shovel!' Lisa pointed to the ancient tools propped against the wall. The shaft of the shovel splintered and broke in two the moment she picked it up.

Dead man's hands, dead man's sweat and toil. Kirstie shuddered. *I said, don't think about it!* she told herself. 'Lisa, there's a pair of iron wheels up ahead!'

'Yeah!' Lisa's lamp lit up the remains of the cart John must have used to carry the rocks containing silver ore. 'Why are we whispering?'

'Don't ask me!' Kirstie hissed.

They laughed nervously and forced themselves onwards down the slope.

'He made this tunnel pretty good!' Lisa pointed out the sturdy props made from the plentiful pines growing on the mountain. Even after all these years, they carried the weight of the roof without strain in the stretches which the miner had judged to be less stable.

'Remind me not to look up any more!' Kirstie wiped a splash of freezing water from her face. 'How long have we been down here?'

Lisa peered at her watch. 'Five minutes.'

'Watch out for this pile of rocks!' Kirstie had stumbled against them and was now picking her way around. Ahead, she saw two ridges of metal laid on to wooden sleepers; a primitive railtrack constructed for the rock-bearing cart.

Dead man's muscle. Dead man's determination to rip precious metal out of the belly of the mountain.

'Is it me, or is the roof getting lower?' Lisa stopped at the heap of debris with her head and shoulders stooped.

'It's getting lower,' Kirstie confirmed. 'But anyway, I think I can hear water ahead, which means we must be getting closer to the river . . . unless it's an underground creek, which would be bad news . . . and I can't see any glimmer of daylight . . . just more railtrack . . .' She talked as much to herself as to her companion, trying to keep up her courage as she went.

'But at least we can follow the rail on our way back with Danny, so there's no danger of us getting lost if we happen to come to any forks in the way . . . like here, for instance . . .' She paused at the parting of the ways and heard the rush of water grow louder still. 'Yeah, that's definitely an underground stream, dammit! How long have we been down here now, Lisa? . . . Lisa?'

Kirstie turned her head to aim the yellow beam of light back along the route she'd just come. Rough walls, water dripping from the roof, the buckled, rusty rail. But no Lisa stumbling and stooping after her. Except for the spiders and the other creeping, underground creatures, the miner's tunnel was deserted.

9

'Kirstie, help!' Lisa's voice was faint but frantic. 'I'm down here! Help me quickly!'

Kirstie was running back towards the heap of rocks which half blocked the tunnel. 'What happened? Where are you?' she cried.

The yellow glow from her head lamp wasn't strong enough to pick out detail beyond the rubble. What was worse, the tunnel walls absorbed and distorted sounds, so that now the rush of running water seemed to be everywhere and the girls' voices got sucked into it.

'Here! I can't get out!'

Scrambling around the loose rocks, heaving the smaller ones aside, Kirstie traced Lisa's position. 'Keep talking!' she urged. 'Let me know if I'm on the right track.'

'Come this way. I can see your light. I knocked mine out when I fell . . . Yeah, right around the rocks . . . I took a different route to the one you chose. I'm down this crevice . . . Stop right there!'

Kirstie halted. She crouched at the edge of a fissure of rock and peered down it. The crack was even darker than the rest of the tunnel, but eventually she could make out the pale shape of Lisa's face. When she directed her light towards her friend, she could see terror in her wide eyes. 'OK, don't move!' she whispered.

'Kirstie, you gotta get me out!'

'I will. Listen, Lisa, are you standing on something firm and safe?'

'I don't know. I think so. One leg hurts like hell. And it's wet down here. I'm in some kind of creek up to my knees, and it's icy!'

'Right. I'm gonna use a rope to pull you out.' Kirstie moved fast. She recognised the danger of Lisa losing her foothold and slipping even further into the water, where the undertow might be strong enough to sweep her off her feet. So she uncoiled the rope which she had slung over her shoulder and made a rough noose. 'When I lower this to you, put it around your waist. OK?'

Lisa nodded. Her breathing came in short gasps as she reached out to grab hold of the noose.

'Can you do it?'

'Wait . . . yeah! What now?'

'Try to take some weight on the leg that doesn't hurt!' Kirstie was looking round for a way of dragging Lisa out of the fissure, realising that the surface of the rock would be wet and slimy, and that there was a real risk of them both being dragged down the hole and out of sight. Her eyes lit on a thick prop supporting the roof nearby, and she backed off towards it.

'Kirstie, don't leave me!' Lisa panicked as the beam of light above her head vanished.

'I'm still here. I'm running this rope around a vertical roof support, so it can act as a kind of pulley . . . almost ready!' She crunched over loose rubble, stumbling and nearly letting go of the rope. She recovered, slung it around the upright prop and came back in Lisa's direction. Then she wound the end of the rope around her own waist, ready to take the strain. 'OK, when I give the word, you have to ease yourself out of there! Ready?'

'I can't see you! What are you doing?' Lisa cried.

'No time to explain. Trust me. Just tell me you're ready to feel the rope go tight!'

'Yeah, ready!'

So Kirstie dug in her heels and leaned back. The rope creaked and strained, chafing at the rough surface of the wooden prop. She pulled harder, stepping back inch by inch. 'How're you doing?' she yelled.

'Yeah, it's working!' In the faint beam of Kirstie's light, Lisa's face appeared at the rim of the fissure. 'A little bit more!' she begged.

Still straining, leaning back with all her weight, Kirstie pulled. A couple more inches, and Lisa would be able to use her arms and shoulders to haul herself out.

'OK, that's enough!' Emerging up to her waist, Lisa wriggled free of the crevice like a swimmer climbing out of a pool. Then she lay flat on her belly, half gasping, half crying, while water streamed off the lower half of her body.

Kirstie unwrapped the rope from her waist and ran to her. She took off her own jacket and wrapped it around Lisa's shoulders, helping her into a sitting position. 'Which leg?' she asked, rubbing her arms to keep her warm.

Shuddering, Lisa pointed to her right ankle. 'Not broken,' she insisted. 'I twisted it as I went down. Oh gee, Kirstie, what an idiot! I'm real sorry!'

'Yeah, just don't ever give me a shock like that again, OK?' Kirstie loosened Lisa's noose and slipped the rope down around her ankles, noticing that the right one was already swelling. 'We've gotta get you out of here,' she decided.

'No!' Suddenly Lisa's voice changed. It grew louder, more determined. 'I mean it, Kirstie. We came down here to rescue Danny Boy, remember? And no way is a twisted ankle going to stop us!'

'You can't carry on like that.'

'Yeah, but *you* can!' Lisa's eyes gleamed as she sat huddled under Kirstie's jacket, knees drawn up to her chest.

'Alone?' Kirstie glanced down the tunnel, then back up the way they'd come. 'You'd have to wait here for Danny and me to come back. It'd be totally dark. No, really; I gotta take you back to Hadley!'

'I said, no way!' Reaching forward, Lisa took hold of Kirstie's wrist. The dark pupils of her green eyes narrowed in the direct glare of the lamp. 'I'll be fine, I promise. And besides, I would never, ever forgive myself if we had to leave Danny behind!'

So the plan was for Kirstie to follow the rusted rail track until it came out by Big Bear River.

'Even if it doesn't come out on Danny's ledge, at least we'll know. And we'll have done everything we could!' Lisa had insisted. 'Go, Kirstie; please!'

'Ten minutes max!' Kirstie had promised.

Ten minutes which could mean the difference between life and death for Danny Boy.

She walked into the dripping darkness, towards the growing roar of the river beyond.

Follow the sound! she told herself. Terrifying as it was to hear the swollen river grow louder, at the same time she knew that it meant she was nearer to Danny's ledge.

But the tunnel seemed to be wetter, the slope downwards steeper. And she was definitely wading through water. Kirstie paused to look down at her feet. By this time, the stream was picking up small pebbles and rushing them along, eroding the floor of the tunnel so that the wooden sleepers laid by Miner John were displaced and the metal rails twisted. Still, she must follow them.

Glancing up again in the direction she had to follow, she thought she saw a faint glimmer of light; the tunnel's end.

With this hope, she gathered her courage. She even raised her voice to call out Danny's name.

'Da-nneee! Da-nneee-Bo-oy!' The shaft distorted it and threw back an echo.

Her feet splashed through the channel of freezing water. More light ahead; a definite easing of the darkness.

'Da-nneee!'

This time, she stood still and tried to pick out an answer through the sound of the water.

There it was! So faint she thought at first that she'd imagined it. She listened again. Yes; a whinny from Danny Boy. Enough to make her plunge on down the slope.

'I'm coming!' she promised, staggering over a piece of twisted track, talking to herself to keep her courage up. 'If Miner John and Jethro could do this week after week, through winter and summer, then so can we!'

Stumbling, slipping, sliding in and out of the stream, promising Danny that nothing now could stop her from rescuing him from the ledge, she came up against . . . solid blackness!

'What?' Kirstie cried out, bewildered. She fumbled for her head light, flicking its switch on and off to no effect. Then she fingered the glass disc, found that it was broken and concluded that she must have knocked the light against whatever obstacle she had just come up against. So she was without light, and there was a wall blocking her way. Or not so much a wall as an old rock-fall, to judge by the loose rubble.

But, however it had come there, it blocked the route leading to the exit of Miner John's tunnel. From the floor to within a foot of the low roof, there was a pile of huge rocks that were impossible to pass by.

Yet there had been light; more than the narrow

grey shaft filtering through the shallow gap. And this mountainside was riddled with more holes than Swiss cheese, Kirstie reminded herself with grim determination. What if she were to backtrack and check for side tunnels? That was possible. Miner John had worked this seam for a long time, probably blasting out tributaries from the main shaft in the obsessive drive to uncover new veins of silver.

Yes! She wouldn't give in! Even without her light, she could feel her way back up the slope until she found one of those secondary tunnels.

Dropping to her hands and knees, feeling the running water swirl around her wrists, Kirstie backtracked.

'So near!' she whispered. The river sounded only feet away, but all around her, so that if it hadn't been for the slope of the tunnel, she would have lost her bearings. Up a few yards on her hands and knees, hoping for daylight filtering down a previously ignored side shaft. A few yards more, feeling her way, her ears filled by the grind of pebbles washed by the water against the iron track, and the roar of white rapids in the river below.

Then, yes! The thing she was praying for; a side shaft sending the faintest glimmer, and a rough, narrower opening which led down again in the direction she needed to go. Still crawling, soaked to the skin and freezing to the bone, she went down it.

More light! For sure! Less grey, more white.

Hope swelled from the tiny grain she'd kept hold of in her heart. 'I'm coming, Danny!' she muttered.

Rising to her feet, steadying herself against the tunnel wall, she kept her gaze fixed ahead. There was an arch of light, criss-crossed with moving branches, the crash of the river, the splash of white spray rising from the rocks below.

'Almost!' she promised. Her steps were unsteady, her body shaking.

Daylight dazzled her after the dark journey so that she had to shield her eyes as she came to the exit to the shaft. She pushed aside slim branches of willow bushes and looked out.

There was a six foot ledge, then a sheer drop of twenty feet to the river. To the left, upstream, a sweep of water tumbling over boulders, swirling in foaming green eddies between sheer pink cliffs. Downstream to the right, a promontory and the remains of a wooden sluice striding out from a small pebble beach across the current.

A vertical iron ladder fixed to the cliff led up from the sluice to Kirstie's ledge. She followed it with her eye, almost afraid to examine the platform. Common sense told her: yes, this is Danny's ledge. Everything slots into place; the promontory, the sluice box, Miner John's secret shaft.

But still, as she looked away from the tumbling river, and raised her gaze up the line of the rusty ladder to the far end of the platform, she prayed that she was right.

10

The small black horse stood still as a statue, watching her. Nothing moved; not even the tip of his ears or the rim of his black nostrils. The white star on his forehead shone from the shadow of the deep overhang.

Kirstie took a long breath. Cold air entered her lungs and cleared out the dank heaviness of the tunnel.

'Danny!' she whispered.

The colt's ear flicked. He swished the end of his tail. But he made no move towards her.

They were divided by thorny undergrowth and by willow bushes, whose tall, bare wands bent and rattled in the stiff wind. The same wind raised the long hair of Danny's mane and made his flanks quiver as he stared back at her.

'I made it,' Kirstie said simply.

Danny lowered his head and snorted. His ordeal seemed to have transformed him from the willing young horse who was eager to please into a wary, hostile stranger.

'I told you we wouldn't let you down.' Slowly, smoothly, she began to ease along the ledge, trusting the sound of her voice to keep Danny calm. If he panicked now, feeling that she might be trying to corner him, he would have to either charge straight at her, or veer towards the edge, both of which could prove fatal.

'I need you to be steady and good,' she murmured. 'Remember all that work we did together? What a smart little guy you were! And they all said we wouldn't make a ranch horse out of you. Did we prove them wrong, or what!'

The colt's head went up in fear, his flight instinct thwarted, knowing that all that was left to him was to strike out with his hooves.

Or to accept Kirstie's gentle approach. To recognise that this was his saviour.

'And you want to come back and show them what you can do,' she went on, edging closer still. She could almost reach out and take hold of the trailing reins, if she dare risk stooping and exposing the back of her head and neck to those feet. No; better to move in close and run the palm of her hands over his shoulders, let him get used to her again. Once he trusted her, he would let her lead him.

But his head kept on going up and he rolled his eyes. He jerked sideways, away from her towards the cliff edge, pulled himself up, called out a warning for her not to come too near.

Up on Mountain Lion Ridge, from the shelter of the culvert, Lucky called back with a long and piercing neigh.

Danny Boy's ears flicked this way and that. He called again and once more got a reply from the ridge above.

'That's Lucky,' she reminded him. 'I bet he's telling you to get a move on. He's cold waiting up there, and it's gonna snow before the day's out . . .'

144

Danny lowered his head, making a chewing motion with his bottom jaw. He took his first step towards Kirstie.

'Yeah, see! Even if you don't want to listen to me, you've got old Lucky handing out the orders!' *Better!* she thought. *Soft eyes, soft hands.* Soon the colt was walking right up to her, nudging her arm, asking her to lead the way.

So she picked up the rope, stroked the youngster and soothed him some more. She was about to take him and show him the way from the ledge when she spied the saddle she'd taken off him, pushed to one side. 'How do you fancy doing your share of the work around here?' she queried, stooping once more, but this time to lift his leg. 'Was this the one that you were limping on? Well, how is it now? Let me look. Easy, boy!'

Obligingly Danny Boy bent his knee. She checked the joint but couldn't see any swelling, or too much wrong with the whole leg except for the cuts sustained in the fall. Deciding to risk it, she quickly saddled him and tightened the cinch, being careful to tuck up the broken stirrup so that it didn't clunk and bash against his side. Then they were ready to leave.

But it was a cave leading into a tunnel; exactly the kind of space a young horse hated. Kirstie felt Danny hesitate as she eased him along the ledge.

'OK, so this is like going into a truck,' she reminded him, not trying to force him, but instead stroking him and talking him through it. 'It's kind of closed in and not very nice, I agree.'

But better than staying here and freezing in the snow! Surely the nervous colt would realise that.

'C'mon!' she urged. 'Lisa must be going crazy in there waiting for us!'

Reluctantly he went forward, almost rearing once, as she tried to lead him through the willow branches. He tugged hard at the rein, but the noseband on Ben's specially constructed bosal tightened and reminded him to fall into line. So he steadied and moved on into the tunnel.

And this, despite the relief of finding a way out for Danny Boy, was the part Kirstie was dreading; the return underground, through the dripping dark passageways blasted out of the rock by Miner John. Uphill this time, until they rejoined the main shaft, leaving behind the very last of the daylight.

As she led Danny, she felt her breathing grow shallow. The blackness was like a cloth over her face, almost suffocating her as she tried to feel her way forward by testing her footsteps along the side of the buckled and twisted railway track. She sensed Danny hesitate too, as if every nerve ending resisted the journey, and when she stumbled, he shied away.

Feeling the rein slip through her hand, Kirstie held tight at the last moment. Dreadful to lose hold now and have them both floundering to find each other in the pitch dark.

But some instinct seemed to take over in the colt. Perhaps he had a sure idea that the incline would take him to freedom, a sixth sense that brings lost animals home and which is a source of wonder to humans. Or maybe he was surefooted simply because horses have good night vision. No yellow head lamp wobbling faintly over the rough walls and rocky floor was necessary for *him* to pick his way. In any case, he plodded steadily on.

Their footfalls splashed and crunched up the

slope in the otherwise silent tunnel. Far behind now, Big Bear River poured down the narrow chasm between the pink granite rocks.

Ahead, a querulous voice called Kirstie's name.

'Yeah, Lisa, we made it!' Up as far as the first rock-fall, persuading Danny through the narrower gap, making him stop to take on a passenger.

'I can walk!' Lisa protested, heaving herself to her feet, then crying out in pain as she tried to take her weight on her injured ankle.

'Sure you can!' Kirstie fumbled for Danny's good stirrup and waited for her friend to hop alongside. She helped ease her up on to the colt's back. 'How far is your head from the roof?' she asked.

'A couple of inches. Ouch! . . . Less, I guess!'

'OK, lean forward when Danny sets off. You can rest your weight against his neck; he won't mind.'

Ready for the final stretch, her lungs aching for fresh air again, Kirstie moved the horse on.

And on, with the river's roar lessening, the glimmer of daylight ahead, the rising certainty that they were going to make it . . .

'What kept you?' Hadley demanded as they

emerged from the cave at the base of Monument Rock.

They were injured and frozen, dirty and scratched, half scared out of their wits. But they had Danny with them. The old wrangler had levered open Miner John's secret door, but now it had creaked shut behind them and they stood on the icy ledge, blinking at the broad daylight.

'That fifteen minutes turned into more like thirty five,' the old wrangler complained. 'Here I am, reckoning you were gonna make me come right in there and fetch you out myself!'

'Some nerve!' Lisa grinned, nursing her twisted ankle on a raised pillow on a couch in the living-room at Half-Moon Ranch. 'My bet is, Hadley wouldn't even have dared set foot in that tunnel!'

'How d'you figure that one?' Leaning on the windowsill, Kirstie watched Luke, Darren and the other vacation operators shake hands with Sandy and Matt as they stepped into the mini-bus which was to drive them to Denver airport.

'He said it himself,' Lisa explained. 'When they were kids, they never looked too hard for Miner John's claim because they were all spooked by the headstones on the hill. I bet he still thinks there are ghosts up there!'

'Hadley's tough.' Kirstie turned in towards the room with the big log fire and the patterned rug. She doubted Lisa's theory, but only argued lazily. After all, it had been a hard day.

'Tough, but scared of ghosts!'

'I'll tell him what you say!' she threatened.

'No, Kirstie!' Lisa swiftly pulled back. She jerked her ankle and gave a yelp.

'Serves you right!' Kirstie turned enquiringly to her mom, who had just come into the hall.

'There goes a bunch of satisfied dudes,' Sandy reported. 'All very happy with the ranch and promising to upgrade us to four diamonds in their lists.'

'Great! Did you call Lorena May to give her the news about Danny?' Kirstie asked.

'I sure did. She said to tell you girls that you did a real good job. Also that she'd love to come back to the ranch and ride again, if we're happy for her to do that. Are we?'

Kirstie swallowed hard. Then she thought about it. After all, Lorena May hadn't done anything wrong exactly. She was actually a good rider, but just inexperienced with cattle. It had been poor judgement that had caused the accident; nothing worse. 'Sure we are,' she told her mom. 'Tell her I'll have Danny ready for her when she decides to come!'

'I'll do that.' Sandy smiled and went out again, humming the opening notes of 'Danny Boy' as she crossed the porch.

'Will you be OK if I just slip out to see Danny?' Kirstie asked Lisa, putting on her jacket.

'Jeez, yes!' Lisa waved her away. 'My mom's due here any moment to drive me home. And drive me *crazy* at the same time, I expect!'

Kirstie laughed. 'She worries about you!'

'Yeah, well. Say hello to Danny for me!' Sinking back against a cushion, Lisa flicked the TV remote to enjoy the last few minutes of pre-Bonnie peace and quiet.

And Kirstie stepped out of the porch and crossed the yard, taking up the strains of the old song too. Maybe it was the full moon sailing from behind clouds, or the feathery snowflakes just starting to drift down; definitely something about the evening made her want to sing.

Up on the hill, the lights of Brown Bear Cabin

were lit and smoke rose from the chimney. That was Hadley holed up cosy and warm. And across the yard, the barn door was tight shut, protecting Danny Boy from the snow and the wind. Lifting the latch and slipping inside, she found Matt, Ben and Charlie all busy shifting bales of hay, stacking them ready to take out to the mangers first thing in the morning.

'Nice song, Kirstie!' Ben called from high up among the bales. 'Say hi to that colt from me!'

'What?' She'd been in a world of her own. 'Oh yeah, I will!'

Danny was in the stall furthest from the door. Ben had bedded him down in the deepest straw, put a rug over his back and dabbed a medication cream on his cuts. Every possible care had been taken to help him over his ordeal.

'See, you're gonna be fine!' Kirstie murmured.

The colt's feet rustled in the straw as he came over to have his nose rubbed.

'Better than a cold cave under Mountain Lion Ridge, huh?' Kirstie petted him and cooed over him, basking in the safety and silence of the barn. No raging river, no hungry predators. Just a haynet hanging from the wall and the smell of clean straw.

'You know who we have to thank?' she whispered, suddenly recalling an object she'd slipped into her jacket pocket by Monument Rock. She pulled it out now to show Danny Boy.

'You see this? This is Jethro's shoe. Jethro was a mule, way back.'

Perhaps expecting something to eat, Danny nudged the shoe with his nose.

'Jethro is who we have to thank for working out a way to get you off that ledge,' Kirstie explained, finding a nail to hang the shoe from on the front of Danny's stall. It looked good. She decided she would like to keep it there as a memento. 'Well, maybe not Jethro himself, so much as his owner,' she corrected herself.

'Miner John is who we have to thank for digging that mine. He was this old guy who found a seam of silver up above Mountain Lion Ridge . . .'

'. . . Who never told a single soul where he staked his claim!' Matt's voice continued.

'. . . And even though claim jumpers followed him, they never discovered the secret door into his mine!' Charlie added.

Blushing, Kirstie turned around and looked up at the haystack. Matt, Charlie and Ben had left off work to listen in to her conversation with a horse. Now they stood in a row, hands on hips, grinning down at her.

'. . . And that door stayed a secret for a hundred years!' Ben finished the story for her. 'Until Kirstie Scott came along.

'So that's who we have to thank for saving your life, Danny Boy. And don't let nobody ever tell you no different, you hear!'

HORSES OF HALF-MOON RANCH
Little Vixen

Jenny Oldfield

Brad Martin, a famous reining expert, visits Half-Moon Ranch with his champion horse, Little Vixen. Kirstie adores the horse but suspects the man. Her worry turns to alarm when a sudden fire traps Little Vixen in the barn. Is Martin to blame? If so, why would he put his own horse in danger? Kirstie aims to untangle the truth from the lies . . .

HORSES OF HALF-MOON RANCH
Jenny Oldfield

0 340 71616 9	1: WILD HORSES	£3.99	❑
0 340 71617 7	2: RODEO ROCKY	£3.99	❑
0 340 71618 5	3: CRAZY HORSE	£3.99	❑
0 340 71619 3	4: JOHNNY MOHAWK	£3.99	❑
0 340 71620 7	5: MIDNIGHT LADY	£3.99	❑
0 340 71621 5	6: THIRD-TIME LUCKY	£3.99	❑
0 340 75727 2	7: NAVAHO JOE	£3.99	❑
0 340 75728 0	8: HOLLYWOOD PRINCESS	£3.99	❑

All Hodder Children's books are available at your local bookshop, or can be ordered direct from the publisher. Just tick the titles you would like and complete the details below. Prices and availability are subject to change without prior notice.

Please enclose a cheque or postal order made payable to *Bookpoint Ltd*, and send to: Hodder Children's Books, 39 Milton Park, Abingdon, OXON OX14 4TD, UK.
Email Address: orders@bookpoint.co.uk

If you would prefer to pay by credit card, our call centre team would be delighted to take your order by telephone. Our direct line *01235 400414* (lines open 9.00 am–6.00 pm Monday to Saturday, 24 hour message answering service). Alternatively you can send a fax on *01235 400454*.

TITLE		FIRST NAME		SURNAME	

ADDRESS	
DAYTIME TEL:	POST CODE

If you would prefer to pay by credit card, please complete:
Please debit my Visa/Access/Diner's Card/American Express (delete as applicable) card no:

Signature .... Expiry Date: ....

If you would NOT like to receive further information on our products please tick the box. ❑